Secret of the Night Ponies

Secret of the Night Ponies

JOAN HIATT HARLOW

SCHOLASTIC INC.
New York Toronto London Auckland
Sydney Mexico City New Delhi Hong Kong

ISBN 978-0-545-28822-4

12 11 10 9 8 7 6 5 4 3 2 1   10 11 12 13 14 15/0

Printed in the U.S.A.   75

First Scholastic printing, September 2010

Book design by Michael McCartney
The text for this book is set in Berling LT.
Excerpt from "October Journey" from *Around the Red Land* by Larry Small, published by Breakwater Books, Ltd., 2007.

This one's for Jackson—age two—
with love and hugs from Noanie

TABLE OF CONTENTS

Easier now to ignore yesterday's universe
Than confront the kaleidoscope of images . . .
Horses hauling their heavy loads
Their bells an octave
In the morning frost
While my father studied trees for timber.
What now, with the horses gone?

—An excerpt from "October Journey"
in *Around the Red Land* by Larry Small

CHAPTER 1

Cries in the Night

A-ROOOOO! Above the wind—a howling, like a wolf baying at the moon! I shot up in my bed, listening. *A-ROOOOO!* There it was again!

When a dog yowls at night, someone is going to die. Shaking, I put my bare feet on the cold floor and headed for my older brother Erik's room and then decided against it. "This is 1965," he'd say. "Don't tell me you still believe those old Newfoundland pishogues, Jessie. They're silly superstitions."

A-ROOOOO! This time the howl turned into a bark, and I knew it was Blizzard, our Newfoundland dog. We sometimes let Blizzard stay outside at night, curled up with his tail around his nose.

"Jessie Wheller!" Dad called. "Shut your dog up! His barking is waking us."

"Yeah! We're trying to sleep," Erik groaned from his room.

"I'll bring him in, Dad," I answered. I lit the lantern on the bedroom table and tiptoed down the stairs, carrying the light ahead of me. Long shadows fluttered around on the walls and floor from the flame inside the lamp. Blizzard yowled again. Why was he crying like that? I asked myself. Something had to be wrong.

Blizzard must have known I was coming because he was scratching and pawing the door. I yanked the handle and nearly fell backward as the door gave way to the wind. The porch was piled with drifts of snow. "Come on in, Blizzard," I said. I held up the lantern and Blizzard's eyes glistened at me. He was standing with a worried look on his face, and his head tilted quizzically. "Come in, boy," I said again.

But my dog headed down the steps and into the deeper snow. He looked back at me again and barked anxiously.

"What's the matter?"

Blizzard wagged his long, wet tail and started off toward the meadow—stopping, looking back, and then barking again.

"Stop that!" I yelled. "Get back in here."

Blizzard sat down right where he was, held his head up high, and yowled. He wanted me to follow him for some reason. But I wasn't about to go out into a snowstorm dressed only in my nightgown. I went back inside to change into warm clothes.

Should I tell Dad where I'm going? I wondered. *No.* Dad had worked hauling wood all day, and I knew he was right tired. And Mom would make me stay in and wait until morning.

I dressed quickly, and then, remembering the new flashlights my cousin Sandra had sent me from the States, I took one from the drawer and turned it on.

Once downstairs I pulled on my boots, then headed out into the storm. "Now, what is it that has you all afire?" I asked Blizzard, who was waiting nervously.

Leaping and struggling in the drifts, he headed toward the east. Where was he going? There was nothing out there. I followed him, pulling my scarf up over my nose to keep the spattering snow from stinging my face. Suddenly I stopped dead in my tracks. Blizzard was leading me to the edge of Devil's Head, the rocky crag that plunged three hundred feet or more to the sea.

"No! Come back, Blizzard!" I yelled frantically.

Blizzard turned and raced back to me. Tugging the sleeve of my jacket with his teeth, he dragged me closer to the edge.

"Help! Help!" cried voices from far below the precipice. Except for the chute, a narrow, dangerous trail, the cliff was a wall of sheer rock. Who could be down there on this stormy night?

I flashed my light on Blizzard, who continued to bark wildly at the rim of the chasm.

Cautiously, I moved closer. "Hello!" I yelled. "Who's there?"

"Help us!" a man called from below. "We're shipwrecked. And we're freezing!"

"Is there a path we can climb?" came another voice.

"It's too dangerous!" I flashed the light down the rocky wall, and I could make out people at the bottom of the cliff. "I'll get help. How many of you?"

"Three!"

"I'll bring my father and brother!" I yelled.

"Hurry!" came the response. "The tide's coming in. We can't last much longer."

"There's a cave just above you on that rocky trail!" I screamed over the roaring of the wind. "Try to get into the cave!" I flashed the light at the cave opening, which was several feet above the shoreline where the group was huddled.

"We see it! Please! Get help quickly, or we'll die!"

I turned to rush back for help, slipping and sliding in my struggle through the deepening snow. Blizzard hesitated to leave the voices at first, but then he came running and was soon ahead of me, barking as he leaped through the drifts.

"Oh, please, God," I prayed breathlessly. "Help us to get back in time to save those people."

CHAPTER 2

Trapped at Devil's Head!

Once inside the house I flew up the stairs. "Wake up, everyone!" I screamed. "There's a shipwreck!"

My mother opened the bedroom door. "What's going on?"

"Blizzard took me to the cliff. There are folks down there shipwrecked, and they're wet and freezing."

Dad was already pulling on his heavy pants over his long underwear. "Get your clothes on, Erik," he said to my brother, who stood sleepily in the hallway. "Quick! Those people can't last long in this weather!"

Mom piled blankets and sweaters into a nunny bag—the waterproof sack Dad used when he traveled by boat. "Go storm the kettle and fill the teapot," Mom ordered me.

I ran to the kitchen, poked the fire, and then poured the steaming water from the kettle into the teapot that was already filled with tea bags for breakfast.

Dad and Erik, who had on their thick gansey sweaters, sat on the kitchen chairs and pulled on their boots. When they ran out the door, Dad had heavy coils of rope over his shoulders and the nunny bag under his arm. Blizzard was pacing back and forth and whining.

Mom stood nearby. "Don't head down into the chute, you hear, Walt? That path is icy, and you'll never make it in the dark. Then who'd come and rescue you?"

My grandmother peered down the stairs. "Did I hear you say Walt's going down the chute?" she hollered. "Has he lost the brains he was born with?"

"Oh, hush, women!" Dad said to them. "Stop your wailing! This is an April storm. The snow will probably be gone by noon. In the meantime we've got to get them up safely." He turned to my mother. "Bertie, you get a hot stew warming. They'll be starvin' when we get back." He patted Erik on the shoulder. "Now you and Jessie get Raven out of the barn. Harness her up to the sled and bring her to Devil's Head."

"No!" Mom said in a huff. "Jessie's not going."

Dad ignored her. "Those folks won't be fit to walk in this snow once we get them up out of the gully. Jessie, you come along and bring them back here on the sled."

He and Erik headed into the meadow, and the beams from their lights bounced in the darkness. Blizzard bounded ahead, barking and howling.

Mom put her hands on my shoulders. "Stay away from the edge of the cliff, Jessie Wheller. Promise me!"

"I promise, Mom."

She sighed, shook her head, and turned to tend the kettle.

I dashed out the door. The snow had let up, and I could see a dying moon peeking between the clouds. Dad and Blizzard were already out of sight.

By the time I reached the barn, Erik had my horse, Raven, bridled and harnessed. Raven threw her head and snorted, her breath making clouds of steam in the cold air. I grabbed one of the larger sleds and attached it to her harness. Erik threw his rope into the sled and hopped on while I hoisted myself onto Raven's back and clicked the reins.

Dad was flashing his light down the side of the cliff when we arrived at Devil's Head. "They're in the cave," he told us. "Let's get these blankets down first. Then we'll figure out how to rescue them."

Erik peered into the dark chasm. "The chute's covered with ice. No one can climb down or up the cliff."

Dad attached his rope to the nunny bag and then went to the edge of the cliff. "We're sending down blankets!" he yelled through cupped hands. He turned to me. "Jessie, you hold the light on the bag as it drops."

I did as I was told and watched as Dad lowered the rope bit by bit. In the bright beam of light I could see someone leaning out precariously from the cave opening and arms reaching up toward the bag as it slipped downward. I held my breath when the bag momentarily snagged on a jut-out of rock. But finally it made its way to the waiting hands at the cave's entrance.

"Thank God!" came a cry from the abyss.

Dad lay on his stomach and looked over the edge. "I'm going down the chute to lead them up," he said finally. "It's the only way to save them that I can see."

"No, Dad!" I yelled. "The chute is all ice. You'll break your neck!"

"At least wait until daybreak, Dad," Erik pleaded. "The spring sun will melt the ice."

"They may not last that long," Dad said.

"You told Mom you wouldn't go down the chute!" I could feel the tears welling up. I knew how dangerous the cliff was, even in the summer on hot, dry days. I looked down at the foaming tidal waves that swirled in circles around the rocks. "Don't go, Dad."

"There's no other way, Jessie. Tie one end of this coil of rope onto my belt. I'll go down, careful-like. Once I get there, I'll fasten the rope to them, one at a time, and they can try to climb up the trail. If they can't, then you hitch the rope to Raven and have her pull each of them slowly up the face of the cliff."

"Don't go, Dad, please."

"Hush, Jessie," Erik whispered. "He's made up his mind."

Blizzard came to me, whining and pawing. I sank onto my knees in the cold snow, knowing right well that nothing I said would change Dad's mind. I buried my face in Blizzard's fur and waited in silence.

CHAPTER 3

Angels or Fairies?

When I peeked out from Blizzard's fur, I saw Erik hitch the cord around Dad's waist. Then Dad disappeared into the chute and down its treacherous trail.

Erik called out every so often, "Are you okay, Dad?"

"I'm fine," came the echoing answer.

I sat shivering next to Blizzard. The only sounds were the wind and occasionally Raven's soft whinny. After ten or fifteen minutes I went to her and put a rug on her back. "Stay warm, Raven," I whispered, patting her nose. "You must be cold just standing here." She snuggled her head against my jacket and whinnied gently.

"Raven has a long fur coat. I'm the one who's about to freeze," Erik complained. "Flat on my belly in the cold snow, ready to fall headlong into an icy abyss." He crept closer to the edge and hollered, "Dad! What's happening?"

"We're coming up the chute," Dad yelled. "There

are two of us. Keep watch and hang on to that rope."

Erik stood up. "Stay close to me, Jessie. Let's haul the rope around that tree," he said, pointing. "It will give us leverage if they fall."

We circled the rope around the tree, and then I stood behind him, bracing my legs as we grasped the thick cable.

"Just hold on. If you feel a big yank, you'll know they're falling. That's when we'll have to pull hard," Erik warned.

Holding our breath, we clung to the rope as it tugged under the weight below. Then, to our relief, Dad's head appeared over the rim of the gorge. He had lost his hat, and he was panting. An elderly man, struggling on the slippery rocks, emerged after him. I could see that the rope was attached to the man and not to Dad.

"Take Mr. Blair home right away, Jessie," Dad ordered breathlessly.

Erik and Dad helped the stumbling, frail man onto the sled where he collapsed. I covered him with a rug, then climbed on Raven's back. "How badly is he hurt?"

"Hard to tell," Dad said. "At least he was able to make it up the chute. We'll know more when he gets to the house. Hurry, Jessie, and then get back here the once." Dad slapped my horse's flank. "Home, Raven!"

Raven tugged forward and then carefully made her way through the snow. It was almost daylight now, and I could see the smoke from our chimney curling upward where the morning star still glistened. "We're almost home!" I yelled to the injured man on the sled. There was no answer. Was he still alive?

Mom must have heard the jingles from the bells on Raven's harness, as she threw open the door. "This man needs help!" I called as I slid off Raven's back.

Mom and I helped Mr. Blair to sit up. He was bleary-eyed and shivering as we half carried him into the house and then practically dragged him to the settle Mom had set up near the stove.

"Once we get you warmed up and some hot tea into you," Mom said, "you'll be fine in no time, Mr. . . ."

"Blair," I said. "He's Mr. Blair."

"Pull his boots off, Jessie," Mom said, "and his jacket. I hope your dad didn't go down the chute. Did he?"

I avoided her gaze and concentrated on the knotted leather ties on Mr. Blair's boots. Mr. Blair smiled weakly as I pulled them off and removed his jacket.

"Jessie, get a cup of tea for this pitiful soul," Mom ordered.

"Before long you'll be too hot, next to this fire," I told him as I poured tea into a mug.

He smiled at me, and his blue eyes crinkled. "Here you are, Mr. Blair," I said. "Be careful now. We don't want you to burn yourself." I lifted him up and held the cup of tea to his lips. "Mom has some good beef stew warmin' up for you."

Mr. Blair sipped on the tea, and then he spoke for the first time to my hearing. "Thank you all for your goodness, especially your little girl here."

Little girl! I was nearly fourteen!

"We're thankful to the good Lord that Jessie found you," Mom said as she spooned a plate of stew from the pot simmering on the back burner.

Mr. Blair looked at me. "Jessie, I do believe you must be an angel, or perhaps one of the little folk— the fairies." His voice trailed off.

Angels? Fairies? Mr. Blair must be a bit bewildered from his experience in the chute, I decided. "I've got to get back to Dad. He'll need me." I got up but stopped before I got to the door. As silently as a phantom my grandmother had appeared, her shiny jet-black hair flowing over the shoulders of her white nightgown.

"Who is this?" she asked, gesturing at our guest.

I knew that if Gran didn't approve of Mr. Blair, she'd make him feel as comfortable as a fish in a net.

"This is Mr. Blair," I said briefly. "Mom will explain everything, Gran. But I've been gone a half hour, and they need me out at the chute." I headed for the door as fast as I could.

CHAPTER 4

Survivors

The storm had passed by the time I got back to
Devil's Head. Dad and Erik were standing with
the two other men who had been in the cave below.
They were younger than Mr. Blair and must have
made it up the chute with less of a struggle. Just the
same, I was glad I had missed the whole ordeal. Dad
had them so completely covered with blankets they
looked like great whales.

"Hurry, Jessie," Dad yelled. "Let's get back to the
house." He helped the two survivors onto the sled,
and I ticked Raven's side with my heel. She plunged
forward in the heavy snow.

"Good horse," I sang to her. "You are my good amazing Raven." Raven snorted and gave her little whinny.
She was winded from her race through the snow, and
her breath came out in rapid white puffs. But I could
tell she was happy to be outside with me.

Off we went again, heading for our house with its
windows shining like gold in the morning sunlight.

Mom was at the open door waiting for us again. "Come in, come in," she said, welcoming my two passengers. "As God would have it you're alive!"

"Your good husband risked his life to save us," said the older of the two, who seemed about Dad's age. "Jessie here told us to climb up to the cave. Lucky we did, 'cause the tide came in a short while later." He climbed awkwardly out of the sled, wrapping the rug around himself. "I'm Donald Anderson," he said with a nod at Mom. "This is my son, Ned."

"That's some sheer drop there at Devil's Head," Ned said. His blanket had fallen from his face, and I realized he was a boy about Erik's age.

Dad and Erik had caught up to us. "You're the only ones to my memory that ever made it to the top— and in a storm at that!" Dad said.

"Come on in now," Mom said again, waving them all into the house. "There's nice hot grub waiting for you. You'll feel good and warm in no time."

Dad and Erik followed Mr. Anderson and Ned into the kitchen. I was about to enter too, but Gran stopped me, her hand on my chest. "Get Raven back to the barn and rub her down right now, Jessie. Then fill up her pail with oats." She let Blizzard into the kitchen but shut the door after him, leaving me standing outside.

"Oh, Gran," I muttered. I never knew what she'd do or say next, for she could change from nice to nasty in a flash. Right now I was mad at her for leaving me outside. But she was right about Raven, who'd been out in the storm since before dawn, so I led my horse to the barn.

"Here I'm the one who went and brought help," I griped to Raven as I removed the rug from her back. I took a towel from a hook and began wiping her down briskly, all the while complaining how tired I was and how I'd been up since two o'clock in the morning. Raven agreed with me, neighing softly and rubbing her head on my shoulder.

The four sheep we had were startled and lowing anxiously to see me in the barn so early in the morning. They stayed together in their stall, their winter coats so thick that they looked like huge snowmen. I threw them a bucket of feed.

Millie Moo, our cow, was becoming full of milk, and she mooed, watching me with big eyes. "Dad or Erik will come soon," I promised her.

After I finished with Raven, I peered out the barn

door. The sun was shining, and the snow was melting fast. Ice candles dripped from the roof, making a trough of slush under the eaves.

I headed back to the house and heard the faint sound of laughter from within.

It sure sounds like our guests have recovered from their close call on the cliff, I thought. *Has anyone even remembered I've been up since two o'clock and had nothing to eat?*

Even Blizzard had abandoned me. I would have gone back to the barn to sulk some more, except I was half starved. So I sloshed through the thawing snow and mud to the kitchen door, kicked off my boots, and went into the kitchen. The room was hot now, with the sun beaming in and the fire still smoldering in the stove. Everyone, except Mr. Blair, was sitting around the table drinking tea and eating biscuits with partridgeberry jam. I could see there was no room for me at the table.

"Come in, maid," Mom said.

"Is there somethin' left for me to eat?" I asked. There was one remaining biscuit on the platter, and I reached out for it.

"That's for our guests," Gran said, pushing my hand

away. "Get yourself a bite from the back kitchen. There's plenty for you out there."

Mr. Anderson spoke up. "Leave her have the biscuit. I'm sure she's hungry. She must be weary, being up all night," he insisted kindly.

"She's young, and youngsters never get weary." Gran nodded at me with a look that meant *Go on now.*

I turned sharply on my heel and headed for the cold, unheated back kitchen where we kept our food.

I found half a loaf of bread and tore off a piece, slapped butter on it, and sat cautiously on the pine chair that had lost rungs and was about to fall apart.

At that moment Mom came in with a cup of tea for me. "Here, Jessie," she said gently. "You must be as hungry as a spring bear. Then come sit with us. We'll make room at the table."

"I don't want to." Suddenly tears sprang into my eyes. I blinked and they tumbled down my cheeks.

"Oh, my child," Mom said, lifting my chin and wiping my tears with her apron. "You're cowed out. Things always seem worse when you're tired."

"I just want to go to bed," I murmured.

"Mr. Blair is asleep in your room, dear. I'm sure

he'll be here for a few days at least, until he's well enough to travel."

I sipped the hot tea and began to feel warmer and sleepier. "Then where will I sleep?"

"Let's see. The boy—Ned, I think is his name—Ned and his father can have the extra room. There are two beds there. And Mr. Blair has your room." Mom thought for a moment. "You can sleep on the chesterfield in the parlor, I suppose."

"But everyone will be walking by and watching me sleep . . . if I'm able to sleep at all, being right there in the parlor."

"Oh, Jessie, these folks were just rescued from a terrible ordeal."

My throat ached, and it was hard to swallow the last bit of bread. I washed it down with the rest of the tea.

"Come along, Jessie. I'll fix the couch up all nice for you." She took my cup and headed back to the front kitchen.

I followed her and nodded at everyone. The young man named Ned was sitting next to Erik.

In the parlor Mom put a pillow and blanket on the chesterfield. I climbed onto the couch, pulled the soft blanket up to my chin, and closed my eyes.

My mind went back to the words Mr. Blair had said about angels and fairies. Perhaps he was so distressed from the ordeal in the chute that he was delirious. Still, I thought about the fairies. Lots of times I had heard Gran talk about the fairies as if they were real.

Was it fairies or angels that spoke to Blizzard so he would rouse me about the shipwreck?

I felt myself sink down, down into the darkness— down into the chute at Devil's Head, down to where the foaming sea swirled in strange circles around the rocks.

CHAPTER 5

Legends of Lonesome Isle

I must have slept for hours. When I awoke, I wasn't sure if it was morning or afternoon . . . or if everything that had happened at Devil's Head had been a dream. And then I saw Ned looking down at me, and I pulled the blanket up over my face.

"Sorry, Jessie. I was just walking by. Didn't mean to wake you," he whispered. Then he asked, "How can you sleep here in the parlor with so many people passing through?"

"Well, I can't now, with you standing over me."

"You've been dead to the world all day and all night, and now it's real early Wednesday morning."

I tried to figure it out. Tuesday morning was the rescue—and now it was Wednesday? "I slept two days?"

"Well, parts of two days."

I peeked out again and saw his face clearly. For the first time I noticed that Ned was right good looking—with a tuft of red hair that toppled over his forehead.

He had a kind smile, but nonetheless, I didn't like to have a stranger peering at me while I was sleeping.

"We were wondering if you were all right. Aren't you hungry? Your mom made fish and brewis. There's a bit left."

"Fish and brewis! And it's not even Sunday? Why didn't someone wake me?" I threw the rug aside and sat up. "I'm starved."

Gran stuck her head around the kitchen door. "Come on, then, maid. There's plenty here for you."

In the kitchen everyone was around the table, except for Mr. Blair. I was still in my clothes from the day before, and I ran my hand over my hair. *I'm all mops and brooms,* I thought, pushing back the mess of strands that had loosened from my long braid.

"How is Mr. Blair?" I asked as I pulled up a chair.

"He's still in bed," Mom answered.

"Indeed." Mr. Anderson nodded his head. "We should have taken him from Last Chance by train, but we thought the boat ride and sea air would be good for him after being cooped up all winter. We didn't expect that squall to blow up."

"He's improving, but I'd feel better if a doctor could examine him," Mom said.

"Nonsense! A trip to the doctor would take more out of him than it's worth. He'll be fine stayin' right here, and I'll see to those bruises. They'll be gone in a week." Gran scooped the fish and crunchy pork brewis from the iron pan into a large plate and handed it to me.

"Why was he leaving Last Chance?" I asked Mr. Anderson.

"Last Chance was his home all his life. But recently we received a telegram from his neighbor there that the old man was not doing well, so we decided to bring him back to live with us in St. John's." Mr. Anderson sighed. "My wife must be worried sick. I wish I could call her. No phones around here, eh?"

"Not yet," Erik answered. "But things'll be changin' once the islanders relocate at Gull Harbor here on the mainland. There'll be so many new people, the government promises to put in roads, electricity, and phones. I'm sure they'll put in phones and lights here, too."

"I can't wait," I said. "I'd love to live near a real city." I was thinking of my cousin Sandra, who lived near Boston in the States. I envied her—so many beautiful clothes, and both her mom and dad had cars.

"Gull Harbor will never be a real city, Jessie," Erik said.

Dad stood up and put his hand on Mr. Anderson's shoulder. "Meanwhile, Don, it's time to get you down to the telegraph office in Gull Harbor. You can send a telegram to Mrs. Anderson back in St John's. We'll go the once, while the tide is in."

"May I go too?" I asked.

"No," said Gran. "Your place is to stay and help out here. Girls shouldn't interfere in men's work."

"Well, God doesn't care if I'm a girl. He used me to get help the other night, didn't he?" I said contrarily.

"Jessie's been wanting to take the boat to the Harbor herself for a long time," Mom explained to the Andersons. "But it's a dangerous trip through those rocks in Stony Tickle, especially when the tide goes out."

"She'd run it up on the sunkers," Erik stated.

I glowered at Erik. "I know my way through Stony Tickle. I'm familiar with every sunken rock—and every hidden ledge. In fact I've even given them names!"

Erik grinned at Ned. "She'd drown us all."

I was so mad I could have clobbered my brother. He had no right to belittle me to Ned. "I'll prove it to both of you!" I snapped.

Ned looked down at the tablecloth and traced a pattern with his finger. "You don't have to prove anything, Jessie," he said softly.

I stood up and started for the door. "Come on. I'll show you right now how well I drive the boat."

"Not in our boat you won't," Erik argued.

Then Dad came to my rescue. "No more glauvaunin' your sister, Erik. She's got to learn how to handle the boat sooner or later. When I go off to the Labrador this year, you're comin' with me, so it's good that she knows her way through the tickle."

"I'm goin' to the Labrador this summer?" Erik exclaimed. "You never said a word!"

"It's time for you to learn the real fishin' trade," Dad said. "And Jessie will soon need to drive the boat herself."

"But . . . ," Erik stammered. "But I needs to teach her."

"You don't needs to teach me. I already know—"

Dad interrupted me. "Stop all this arguin', both of you."

I said no more, but as soon as I had a chance, I was going to show Ned how well I could navigate and drive the boat all by myself.

I went to my room, unbraided my hair, and let it

loose down to my waist, brushing it over and over. Looking in the mirror, I understood again why people often said I favored my grandmother in looks: because of our raven-black hair. My brown eyes were still angry after my jawing with Erik, and that made me look even more like Gran. I plaited my hair in one long braid, then dressed in warm slacks and my heavy cable fisherman's sweater that Gran knit from the wool of our own sheep. It would be cold out on the water.

I joined Dad, Erik, Ned, and Mr. Anderson as they walked beyond the barn to the cove where we kept our boats. Dad had put Raven out in our little pasture, and she ran to the fence when she saw me. I went over to pet her. "My sweet Raven," I whispered. "You're out in the sunshine, and don't you love it?" She nuzzled my shoulder as if to agree. Then, after snorting a few times, she scampered around the paddock through the melting snow and mud, her legs kicking playfully behind her. Once again she came to me, tossing her head, her mane tangled and blowing.

"I know you'd rather be running free, Raven. But the law says all ponies have to be fenced in so you don't trample people's gardens." I scratched her nose. "I'll be back to brush you down."

When I caught up with the men, Blizzard was way ahead of us. However, he stopped and waited for us to catch up. Whenever we headed toward the inlet, he'd get all excited, expecting a ride in the boat.

I took a deep breath of the pine-scented wind and raised my face to the sky. A fish hawk soared above the cliffs, its shadow fluttering along the path. Blizzard jumped after it, and Ned laughed. "You'll never get anywhere chasing shadows, Blizzard," he said. He turned to me. "Blizzard's a Newfoundland dog, isn't he? Yet he's black and white."

"He's a pure-blooded Newf," I told him. "When they're black and white like Blizzard, they're called Landseers."

Our sheltered harbor was on the leeward side of our house, where the water was usually calm—in the opposite direction of Devil's Head. As we headed down the slope to the inlet, I noticed Ned had slowed his pace and was lagging behind. I stopped to wait for him.

"Your brother kept talking about Stony Tickle being dangerous," he said. "Is Erik afeared of this passage to Gull Harbor?"

"He's afeared of me learning the boat and using it myself—that's what he's afeared of!"

"Jessie, just between you and me, after hearin' all the jabber about the rocks in that tickle, I'm a bit nervous," Ned stammered. "Since the shipwreck . . . well, I don't want my dad to know, but . . . that storm was like nothing I'd ever seen. And when I tumbled out of the boat and into those mountainous waves, I thought for sure I was a goner."

"It's no wonder you're ascared, Ned. But we'll be through that stony passage in no time."

Ned pointed to the hilly island to the west. "What's that land out there?"

"That's Lonesome Isle," I told him. "It's been deserted for years."

"It sure looks lonesome," Ned observed.

"My dad grew up out there," I told him. "It's a sad, haunted place. There are hollies out there."

Ned stopped walking. "Haunted? Hollies? Go on with you!"

"Maybe you don't believe me, but everyone around here knows it's true."

"Maybe I'd believe you if I knew what you were talking about," Ned said. "And what are hollies?"

"Hollies are the wails of ghosts," I explained. "Years ago a wicked bad storm blew up, and a steamer on its way to Gull Harbor lost power. The breakers drove it onto the rocks just off of Lonesome Isle. The ship sank, and everyone on board drowned. Whenever there's a gale, they say you can still hear the wails of the folks who were lost."

"Did you ever hear the hollies, Jessie?"

"No! I never go out there. You see, some of the bodies washed up onto the shore of the island— including my grandfather and two uncles."

"Was that your gran's husband?"

"Yes, and my dad's brothers. My grandmother found their bodies herself."

"What a right awful thing. No wonder she left the island," Ned said. "And no wonder she seems . . . well . . . kind of cold."

"Hmm," I said thoughtfully, "Perhaps that *is* the reason she's so cold."

"Someday, when I come back to visit, let's go out to Lonesome Isle to explore."

"Oh, no, Ned! We must never go out there—not in a million years. Neither would anyone else around these parts."

We reached the wharf. Dad and Mr. Anderson had taken the tarp off the boat and checked the engine.

Blizzard was already aboard, and as Ned and I climbed in, he scooted up to the bow, his tail wagging like a flag.

After a few coughs the motor began to purr. Erik unhitched the ropes, and we slowly backed out into the deeper water. Then, slipping around the sandbar that protected the entrance to our little cove, we headed south and away from land.

There were still pans of ice in places around the shore, but they would soon be gone in the spring sunshine. I breathed in the fresh, salty air. I loved setting out in a boat. It was like flying through the wind. I loved the sting of the salt spray on my face. Most of all I loved the sea. I loved the way it glittered in the sunlight. I loved the great mountainous breakers, which filled me with wonder about God and his power.

Across from me Ned was peering down into the black water, where the boulders and ledges lurked. I saw him clutch the gunwale with white, tense knuckles.

Poor Ned, I thought. *I suppose I'd be scarified if I'd been shipwrecked in a squall.* But still and all, despite shipwrecks and wailing ghosts, I knew for certain I would never stop loving the sea. And I knew for certain I'd find a way to show Ned that I was a great sailor.

CHAPTER 6

Reunion at Gull Harbor

Ned seemed more relaxed after we made our way through the tickle and into the waters of Gull Harbor. "That's Cairn Head," I called out, and gestured to three piles of rocks that stood out high on a hill. "It used to be a marker for sailors many years ago."

"What's that island over there?" Ned asked, pointing.

"That's Stepping Stone Island," Dad said. "It will be deserted soon, because the families have decided to take part in the Household Resettlement Program. The government is trying to get people into larger communities. They'll pay them, or help them in some way, to move."

"Lots of folks are floating their houses to the mainland so they don't have to build another," I said.

"They're busy with that project in St. John's," Mr. Anderson told us. "The Department of Fisheries will be giving money to those families who move."

"Kind of puts pressure on people who don't want to leave their homes, doesn't it?" Dad asked.

"I'm sure not everyone will be happy," Mr. Anderson agreed.

"It's sad for those ponies out there," Dad said. "They're just being abandoned. Something should be done to save them before next winter hits."

I thought of Raven. We'd never just leave her . . . no matter what. She was part of our family.

As we pulled into a dock, Dad turned off the engine. "Erik, hitch the boat to the grump heads." Erik hopped out and quickly tied the boat to the tall posts on the wharfs.

I could see kids my age walking up the road in groups, and knew that classes in the two-room schoolhouse were out for the day. I had to be careful not to run into Irene Campbell, the woman who would be my teacher—if I went to school again, that is. She didn't like the idea of me being taught how to read and write by Gran. Whenever Miss Campbell saw me, as quick as you'd say trapsticks, she'd jaw me about my not going to school. I told her I could read and write and sum just fine, thank you. Besides, I'd already tried school a few times, but it was too far to go, especially in winter.

"We're goin' to the telegraph office and the post

office," Dad said to me as the men headed up the road.

"Want to come along?" Ned asked.

"We're stoppin' at the bakery," Erik added.

"No, I'll just mill around and talk to my friend-girls," I said. "I haven't seen the Doyle twins in ages."

"How do you know these girls?" Ned asked.

"Dad used to drop me off on Stepping Stone Island to play with them. We've known them and their families for years," I explained.

Once again Blizzard looked undecided—starting first after Dad, then pausing and gazing back at me.

"Go with Jessie," Dad ordered. Blizzard wagged his tail and trotted to my side.

We walked up the road to where the girls were playing jump rope in front of the church. When they saw me they stopped. "Winter must surely be over! Here's Jessie just out from the Cliffs!" Meta Rideout called as she ran to meet me. Everyone referred to our place as "the Cliffs."

They all hugged me, while Blizzard jumped and wiggled and lapped their hands.

"What are you doin' way out here today?" Polly Doyle asked.

"The sight of you is good for sore eyes," her twin, Trudy, said.

"How long are you stayin'?" asked Meta.

"Just until our new friend sends out a telegram," I told them. "There was a shipwreck near us during the storm early Tuesday mornin'. We pulled three men out of the chute at Devil's Head."

"Good morrow to you!" Meta said, her eyes wide. "No one ever made it up that chute . . . and certainly never in a squall of snow and ice."

"It's the truth, I swear it," I said. "But Meta, tell me about you. Did your folks agree to the resettlement program? Have you moved in to Gull Harbor from Stepping Stone Island already? Here you are . . . yet I can still see your house out there on the point."

"I moved in this winter with Polly and Trudy, so I could go to school. Miss Campbell used to come to our island every six weeks to teach us."

"If it wasn't stormy," Polly interrupted.

"But she doesn't go from island to island anymore," Meta continued. "She teaches full time at the Gull Harbor school."

"Since we've moved to the Harbor, we're real school girls, Jessie," Trudy said. "Our house is being hauled in this weekend. We have a lot of land over there." Meta pointed to a cleared lot near the schoolhouse. "And we've got people with a real bulldozer to pull the house up to the land after they float it over here on Saturday."

"It'll be fun to watch," Polly said.

"I'm glad you'll be closer to me now," I told her.

"Meta's lived with us all winter, and we've had such fun, Jessie," Polly said. "And now we'll be real neighbors again."

"Where did your folks live while you were in Gull Harbor?" I asked.

"They came in when they could—by pony and sled—when the harbor was frozen. But they were the only family out there on Stepping Stone all winter," Meta answered.

"It must have been lonely with no one nearby," I said.

"They were busy getting things ready for the move," Meta explained. "And they fed the ponies that were abandoned."

"Oh, I'm so glad to hear that," I exclaimed. "We wondered how the horses survived. My wonderful, beautiful Raven is one of the Newfoundland ponies.

I can't even dream of leaving her alone on an island. She's part of our family. She knows us and loves us. "

"Well, for now the horses are okay. There was plenty of hay from last summer," Meta said. "But Mom said one night in a storm she heard strange noises. She was some scared, let me tell. She thought there might be ghosts out there."

"What was it?" I asked.

"As it turned out, some of the horses sidled up to the house for protection from the snow." Meta put up her hand. "Now, don't worry, Jessie. Mom and Pop got them to an empty barn the next day. The horses are all right."

"Oh, Jessie, we have some real good news," Polly said.

"Let *me* tell." Trudy elbowed her sister, then turned to me. "We're going to be aunts!"

"Our sister Judy, in Corner Brook, is havin' a baby in June!" Polly added.

Trudy clapped her hands. "Ain't it exciting? We can't wait to visit and see the baby when it comes."

At that moment the girls hushed their talk and nudged each other. I followed their gaze to see little Clara Cadigan, her head bowed, walking slowly up the road. She was as poor and rawny as ever, weighing no more than a periwinkle. Her hair was all mops and brooms, and her worn duckedy-mud coat was so big for her it was trailing in the dirt.

"Hi, Clara," Meta said sweetly.

Clara looked up. "Hi, Meta," she called. Her brown eyes were hollow in her pale face. She smiled and waved, then darted over to us. "Hi, Jessie," she said. "Are you stayin' here for a while?"

"No, Dad's here to send a telegram. How do you like livin' here at Gull Harbor now that you've moved from the island?"

Clara's smile faded, and she just shrugged.

Clara was only about seven. The kids in Gull Harbor pitied her and called her a little angishore—a poor, miserable little girl who looked sad and uncared for. The fact that she lived with the McCrumbs was enough to make anyone miserable, I thought.

"I better go back to the boat," I said. "Mr. Anderson and the men must be done by now."

"Oh." Meta sounded disappointed. "You just got here, and now you're leavin'."

"Come back soon, Jessie," Polly said with a pout on her face.

"Yes, it's always more fun when you're here," Trudy added.

"May I walk down to the wharf with you and Blizzard?" Clara asked. "I'm goin' your way."

"Sure," I replied. The McCrumb house and barn were next to the docks. The barn was old and had been on that property for years. But the house had recently arrived—they'd floated it over from Stepping Stone Island this past fall, when the government promised to pay folks to relocate. It was about that time when the Doyles had moved out, too.

I said good-bye to the others, and then Clara and I headed back to the waiting boat. She held my hand as we walked. "I wish you lived closer, Jessie," she said. "I'm so glad when you come to the Harbor."

"I'll be back tomorrow or the next day, Clara, and I'll bring you a surprise." I was thinking of some of my outgrown clothes that I knew she could use.

We walked down the steps of the wharf, where Dad and the others were waiting. Chet Young, our Mounted Policeman, was on the wharf talking to Dad.

"Hi there, Jessie," Chet said. "Good to see you back in civilization," he teased. I just grinned at him.

Everyone loved our Mountie. He was friendly, but firm when he needed to be.

"Hello, Clara," said Dad, patting Clara's head. "How are you, my child?"

"Fine, thank you, Mr. Wheller."

"This is my friend Clara," I said to Ned. "Clara, this is Ned." Clara gave him a shy smile, then turned to me. "I can't wait for you to come back, Jessie."

"We'll be back in a day or two," Dad told her.

"We're expecting a reply to our telegram," Ned added.

Suddenly, from the road above the wharf, came a call. "Clara! Come home the once, child, and don't bother them folks. You're late and you have chores to do."

Henrietta McCrumb, Clara's guardian, stood at the top of the stairs, a big smile on her face.

"I'm comin', Ma," Clara called. I wasn't surprised to see her pale face turn even paler as she darted up the steps where Henrietta waited. *She's afraid of Mrs. McCrumb*, I thought.

"How are you, Walt?" the woman called to my father. She smiled and waved to us, then put her arm around Clara and led her to their house. I kept watching as

Mrs. McCrumb opened the door and shoved Clara inside. Then, to my horror, Mrs. McCrumb raised her hand, and just before the door shut, I saw Clara cringe and shield her head with her arms.

I ran to my father, who was climbing into the boat. "Did you see that, Dad?" I yelled. "I think Mrs. McCrumb was about to hit Clara!"

"Henrietta was probably just chastisin' Clara for not coming straight home," Dad said. "Calm down, Jessie."

"You've got to get Clara out of that house and away from those people!" I insisted.

"I know the McCrumbs weren't a good choice as parents for Clara," Chet Young replied. "Howsomever, they're probably doin' the best they can."

"I think they're cruel people. Clara shouldn't have to live with them," I repeated.

"Jessie, try not to worry," Chet said. "The McCrumbs will be careful with Clara—if not out of kindness, then out of fear they'll get arrested. I have all these islands plus Gull Harbor on my watch, but if it will make you feel better, I'll keep an extra watch on Clara. It's hard to be everywhere, you know." He waved good-bye and headed up the steps to the main road.

Dad turned to Mr. Anderson. "I don't know how

that couple managed to get Clara. Melloy McCrumb is a barnacle. And Henrietta, his wife, is sweet as honey to your face, but I wouldn't trust her as far as I could toss a quintal!"

A quintal—that's a hundred and twelve pounds, I thought. Dad didn't trust the McCrumbs any more than I did.

Later, as we headed home through the dark waters of the tickle, my mind went back to poor little Clara flinching as Henrietta pushed her into the house. I recalled how Clara took my hand when we walked together and how she looked forward to my coming back to Gull Harbor.

All Clara needed was someone to take care of her and love her. She was scared and lost—just like the abandoned ponies on Stepping Stone Island. Wasn't there some way to help them all? I wondered.

Suddenly my own eyes blurred with tears and I let them fall onto my cheeks and mix with the salt spray of the sea.

CHAPTER 7

"I'll Show You!"

The first thing I did when I got home was to tell Mom that I was sure Henrietta McCrumb was about to hit Clara. "Maybe it looked worse than it really was," Mom said.

I wanted to believe her, but it was hard to put the whole incident out of my mind. Later I gathered together a parcel of clothes that I'd long outgrown, to take to the Harbor on Friday. One of the items was a warm plaid coat with a blue velvet collar and a hat to match. Clara would look so cute all dressed up, I thought.

Mom made pea soup with large hunks of ham for supper, and it was a happy meal, with our guests laughing and counting their blessings at being alive. Even Mr. Blair came down to dinner and ate a big bowl of soup with homemade bread. Gran baked a luscious peach pie from our last can of peaches, and of course she made a pot of tea.

"What about your boat, Don?" Dad asked Mr.

Anderson. "Will you try to recover it sometime?"

"No, she's at the bottom of the sea. There wasn't much left after she banged up on those rocks." Mr. Anderson shook his head. "Walt, I honestly thought I knew the way well enough to keep going all night."

"I didn't help much," Mr. Blair admitted. "Jawin' at him the way I did to keep going. I figured we'd make it back to St. John's by the next afternoon if we didn't go into harbor that night."

"We've been hopin' the government would put up a light on Devil's Head to warn about those rocks," Dad said. "Most folks around here know the danger, but anyone unfamiliar with the waters here . . . well, you know only too well."

"When we get back to St. John's, I'll make a point of getting a light up on that cliff," Mr. Anderson promised.

Mr. Anderson must be a real big shot with the government, I thought.

"Friday is Dr. Desort's day at Gull Harbor. See if you can get him to come out here the once and take a look at Mr. Blair," Mom suggested.

"Those witch hazel soaks I made have helped him," Gran said. "His bruises are fading right out of sight."

"That's true, but he should see a doctor. It's times like this when I wish we had telephones," Mom complained.

"Don't ever send *me* to a doctor. Give me a charmer and a few herbs and that's all I need," Gran insisted.

Mom raised her eyebrows. "A charmer is like having a witch doctor. And herbs? Mr. Blair will need more than herbs."

"If you don't believe in herbs, just take a look at Mr. Blair since I've been treatin' him."

Thursday morning, after breakfast, I put on an old pair of overalls, a sweater, and my hip boots and went to the barn to clean Raven's stall. I always felt good when her stall was clean, with sweet hay spread around. Blizzard sat nearby, watching as I shoveled the manure into a wheelbarrow. Millie Moo and our sheep were outside with Raven. They were all wandering around happily, searching for little patches of grass that were beginning to peek through the mud and bits of melting snow.

Erik was busy cleaning Minnie Moo's stall. Raven's care was mine, because she was considered to be *my* horse.

When the wheelbarrow was filled, I rolled it outside

to a pile we saved for the garden. As I pushed through the door, I banged into Ned, who was about to enter the barn. Some of the manure plopped out and onto his pants and shoes. He looked down at his clothes helplessly and then up at me.

"I'm sorry, Ned," I said. "I didn't see you."

"It's all right," he answered, brushing the manure off his trousers. "Phew! I'll stink all day."

I tried my best not to laugh, but a giggle slipped out anyway. "Sorry. It's not funny, I know."

Ned wiped his hands in a small pile of snow. Then he laughed too. "So, this is what it's like, living in an outport."

"This is it. I know the townies make fun of us, don't they?"

Ned looked embarrassed, then said, "Well, not all townies."

"What does your father do in St. John's?" I asked.

"He's sort of a lawyer for the province. He works with the premier. His office is in the new Confederation Building. What does your dad do?"

"My dad's a fisherman, mostly. In the summer he goes with a crew out to the Labrador. He's gone sometimes for the whole summer."

"So the rest of you stay here alone?"

"From what Dad said yesterday, Erik will be goin' with him this summer. Then Mom and Gran and I will be stayin' here gardening, milking the cow, shearing sheep, and all that stuff."

"No wonder you'll need to learn how to get around in the boat."

"I already do know how. And I know every rock!" I snapped. "I wish people would believe me."

Ned grinned. "Okay, okay! I believe you."

"Well, I don't!" Erik said as he came out of the barn.

Ned shook his head. "Here we go again!"

"I'll show you once and for all." I slammed the shovel into the wheelbarrow and darted toward the dock, where the boat was tied.

"Don't, Jessie!" Erik yelled, but I was already flying down the steps. The boat was uncovered, and I jumped in. Usually I'd have started the engine first, but this time I slipped the ropes from the posts and pushed out before Erik could reach me.

"Come back, Jessie," Erik yelled.

I pulled the choke, as I'd seen Dad do when the engine was cold. Then I pushed the start button, and WHAM! The boat took off full speed ahead, knocking me back into my seat and then onto the floor of the boat.

When I pulled myself up, I was heading directly into the tickle. *I've got to slow down, before I go up on the rocks!* I grabbed the gas lever and yanked it back. Thump! The boat slowed abruptly, this time knocking me forward into the wheel. What a way to show Erik and Ned that I could navigate the boat as well as anyone!

I took a quick glance back to the wharf, where Ned and Erik were gesturing wildly and yelling at me. I couldn't hear what they were saying over the sound of the engine.

But now the motor was running smoothly, and I puttered along nicely, just far enough south to show that I knew what I was doing. However, it was hard to see where the rocks were from where I was sitting. *I better turn back*, I told myself. *They know now that I can run the boat—even though I didn't get off to a great start.*

Slowly, I turned the boat around to head back, when suddenly the engine began to sputter—and it stopped. Now what? I waited a moment, trying to figure out what was wrong.

I tried choking the gas again and pushing the start

button, but nothing was happening. I knew right well that Erik and Ned were laughing at me.

Well, I could always row back. I looked around the deck but didn't see any oars. Erik must have taken them out, and now I was at the mercy of the tide!

"What are you goin' to do now, Jessie?" Erik yelled from the wharf. Sure enough, he and Ned were bent over laughing.

"The engine won't start!" I answered angrily. "Something is wrong with it."

"There's nothing wrong with it!" Erik called. "You're out of gas!"

Oh, no! I'd never thought about the gas. "Come get me, you stupid gommel!" I yelled.

Erik and Ned were already climbing into our little punt and were rowing out toward me with a towrope.

"The boat was uncovered 'cause Dad was goin' to fill it with gas before we headed out to Gull Harbor tomorrow." Erik tried to muffle his laughter but couldn't. Between chuckles he added, "I tried to tell you, but you wouldn't listen, as usual."

"I'll just bet you tried to tell me!" I said, mustering up as much dignity as I could. "And who took the oars out of this boat?"

"They're by the starboard gunwale, if you'd looked!" came Erik's reply.

When we reached the dock, I climbed out and stormed up toward the barn. "Don't you ever speak to me about this again!"

But I knew my brother, and I knew this wouldn't be the last I'd hear of it.

CHAPTER 8

"No Way on Earth"

I went to the pasture and led Raven back to her stall. I found her currycomb and began brushing her mane. "You're my best friend, Raven. I don't have anyone else here at the Cliffs who likes me. All Erik does is make fun of me. And Gran—well, I know she doesn't like me. And now Erik has gone and turned Ned against me too." For a moment I leaned against Raven's neck, feeling her comforting warm coat against my forehead.

Blizzard, who had come into the barn with me, nudged me with his head, as if to say, *I'm here. I'm your friend, Jessie.* I leaned down and patted him.

To my surprise Ned came into the barn looking a bit sheepish. "I'm sorry I laughed at you, Jessie. It was . . . kinda funny to see you so mad and determined and then . . ."

"Then I made a complete gommel of myself and couldn't even run the boat."

Ned sat on a turned-over barrel and watched me

comb Raven's thick winter coat, which had begun to shed. "I heard you say you didn't have any friends here."

"I don't have any friends here at the Cliffs. I do have friends in Gull Harbor, and my best friend-girl is my cousin, Sandra. But she lives in Boston." I pulled fur from Raven's comb and threw it out the door. "Birds make nests from hair," I told him, hoping to change the subject. I tugged at Raven's mane, and she flicked her tail at me irritably. "I'm sorry, Raven," I said, patting her neck. "You had a burr."

"I can tell you love horses. Where did you get Raven?"

"Raven is one of the Newfoundland ponies that have been in our family for years. We think they were first brought here by early settlers from the British Isles. In the winter they work for their keep, but they're usually set free in the summer to roam about. Some have colts. If the foal is from my horse, then I can keep it, or I can sell it—or give it away. That's what everyone does," I explained. "It's sort of a community herd. But then when a horse belongs to someone, they tend it and love it because it's now a member of their family, like Raven." I gave Raven a kiss on her neck. "Raven knows she's got a good home here with us—unlike some of those poor ponies out on Stepping Stone Island."

"After everyone has moved from Stepping Stone Island to Gull Harbor, who'll care for those horses?"

"No one," I answered.

"Hmm. How many horses do you suppose there are?"

"I don't know, but don't you wish someone would steal them away and find a place for them where they'd be taken care of?"

"Sure, but how could we . . . anyone . . . rescue all those horses?" Ned looked thoughtful.

"As long as we're daydreaming, let's rescue little Clara too, and hide her from the McCrumb family."

I sighed. "I wish we could help her *and* the ponies out on Stepping Stone Island."

"I do too," Ned agreed.

We looked at each other for a long time. Then I shook my head. "No, I guess there's no way on earth . . ."

"You're right," he agreed. "No way on earth."

CHAPTER 9

The Meanest Men
in Gull Harbor

It felt like spring the next morning, with the warm sun and smell of sweet earth. So, off we headed to Gull Harbor. Erik, who was driving the boat, gave me a know-it-all grin. I stuck out my tongue at him and hoped he would not tease me for the rest of my life about my little cruise the day before. Of course he'd had to bring it up at supper. Everyone had laughed, but no one mentioned it again.

Dad and Donald Anderson sat together on the bench seat, talking now and then over the sound of the engine. Blizzard sat up in the bow, looking for all the world like the captain of the ship.

Ned didn't seem as nervous this time. How could he with the water shining and rippling in the sunlight like ribbons of silver? "I'm coming back here someday, and we'll go berrying over on that island," he said to me, pointing to Lonesome Isle. "But of course not during a storm when the ghosts are howling."

"You can go berrying there when you come back and the berries are ripe. But I'm not going to rescue you if the ghosts get you." I would miss Ned when he left, and I wished he could stay longer, but I was a little embarrassed to say so. "We'll go berrying when you come back . . . but not out there," I added after a moment.

He grinned at me, and I could feel my face flush again, so I turned away into the breeze.

Erik took a quick glance at me from the wheel and winked. He must have heard Ned's comment, and I knew I was in for heaps and bunches of teasing later.

As we passed Stepping Stone Island, I could see big boats anchored near the Rideouts' white house, which had been pulled from its foundation to the shoreline. "Tomorrow they'll be hauling that house to the new lot at Gull Harbor," I said. "That's when the horses out there will start fending for themselves."

When we landed at Gull Harbor, Mr. Anderson handed Ned some money and said, "Take Jessie and Erik into the bakery and have a bite to eat. When we're finished at the telegraph office, we'll meet you there."

I gathered up the parcel of clothing I'd brought for

Clara, and we headed up the steps to the dirt street. Blizzard trotted ahead of us, pausing to sniff now and then or bark at a bird.

"Soon the road will be paved, now that so many people have moved here from the islands," Erik told Ned. "Then there will be cars and telephones and electricity . . ."

"And Jessie will have her big city," Ned teased, nudging me.

We found a table near the window, where we could watch Blizzard, who lay on the porch near the door, and then we placed our orders.

The warm sun beat through the glass, and I took off my heavy gansey and placed it on an empty chair along with the parcel for Clara. I looked up and suddenly realized that Molloy McCrumb was sitting at a nearby table with a man I recognized as Jack Hawley. They were deep in discussion, their heads so close their noses almost touched.

"I wonder what evil they're up to," I whispered to Erik and Ned.

"I suspect they're findin' a way to bamboozle someone," Erik said.

Mrs. Chase, the owner of the bakery and wife of

the postmaster, brought us freshly baked muffins with butter and applesauce. The hot chocolate was topped with thick cream.

We hadn't finished when the door opened and Clara came in, still wearing her long dirty coat. She didn't see us but went straight to her foster father. "Ma says she needs you to come home right away. She can't open the cellar door."

Melloy McCrumb was obviously angry at being disturbed. "Course she can't open it, the fool woman. I've locked it!"

"Well, I guess she wants the key, then," Clara said, backing away.

"Can't you get the message right?" he yelled. "Does she want the key or not?"

"I . . . I don't know," Clara stammered. "Tell me where the key is, and I'll give it to her."

"That's not for you to know, you little brazen chit."

Clara cringed and her mouth quivered as he pushed her aside and headed out the door, shutting it with a slam.

Through the window I could see Melloy McCrumb stomp across the porch, then trip over Blizzard, who was sleeping near the steps. I gasped and jumped up from my seat as the man kicked my dog with his big boot and then marched off down the street. Blizzard yelped and scooted away from his spot in the sun.

"Did you see that?" Ned exclaimed. "He kicked your dog!"

"He's a beast of a man," Erik said angrily.

For a moment Clara looked lost as if not knowing what to do, and then her gaze fell upon us. Her face brightened as she came to our table.

"Hi, Clara," I said, holding my arms out to hug her.

"Jessie, I'm so glad to see you again." She fell into my arms and clutched me as if I might disappear. "Hi," she said, peeking out shyly at Erik and Ned.

"Hi, Clara," Erik and Ned answered at the same time.

"I have somethin' for you," I said, reaching for the parcel of clothes. "Want to see?"

We opened the package, and I pulled out the plaid coat and hat first. Clara's eyes lit up like stars when she saw the outfit.

"Let's try it on," I said, unbuttoning the worn coat she was wearing. I helped her into the newer, warmer coat and then tucked the matching hat over her uncombed hair. "There! You look beautiful!" I said. "Can you see your reflection in the windowpane?"

Clara stood as if entranced at her image in the window. "Is this for me to keep?"

"Aye, they're for you," I told her. "And look, here's a little spring dress and sweater you can use for church on Sunday." I unfolded a pink dress covered with tiny green flowers and a matching green sweater. I held it up to her. "You'll look like Cinderella in this, Clara."

Just then the door opened, and Melloy McCrumb stormed into the shop. "What are you doin'?" he yelled at Clara. "Stop botherin' them folks."

I felt my blood rushing to my head and was about to snap back at him, but Ned spoke up instead. "She's not a bother."

I nodded. "We love Clara."

"And one more thing—if our dog is in your way, walk around him. Don't ever kick him again," Erik said boldly.

Melloy McCrumb's eyes darkened, and for a moment I was afeared of what he might do. Then, to my surprise, his whole manner changed, and his mouth stretched into a grin. "Well, Clara, these folks seem to have taken to you." He looked her up and down and touched the collar on her coat. "And they brought you some nice things, I see. Did you say thank you?"

"She already thanked me." I could see relief in Clara's face.

"Now you take your nice things home," Melloy McCrumb told her. "Show 'em to your Mom and let her put 'em away so's they don't get dirty."

Clara nodded and I could see fear again in her eyes. "Good-bye, Jessie," she mumbled, and gathered her things together, including the duckedy-mud coat that I wanted to throw away.

"Good-bye, Clara," I said as she went out of the bakery.

Melloy McCrumb turned away and sat once again with his pal Jack Hawley. He whispered something to Jack, and the two of them looked over at us with dark glances.

I had a strong feeling we had made enemies of two of the meanest men in Gull Harbor.

CHAPTER 10

Fun with Friends

From the window I could see Dad and Mr. Anderson walking toward the bakery. Mr. Anderson had a yellow envelope in his hand. He'd received a telegram! They both stopped to pat Blizzard as they entered the bakery. Blizzard looked up and wagged his tail.

My Blizzard is the sweetest and most loving dog in the world, I thought. *Everyone loves him—except Melloy McCrumb.* Had he ever kicked Clara? I shivered at the thought.

Dad and Mr. Anderson pulled up chairs and sat down. "Here's the reply from my wife, Dulcie," Mr. Anderson said, opening the telegram.

```
Praying that you are all well and
survived without injuries STOP I
hope Pop will be OK STOP Get him to a
doctor soon STOP Trains leave White
Falls to St. John's twice a day STOP
Can someone get you there STOP The
premier was concerned about the
```

```
shipwreck and said to take your time
coming home STOP I miss you all STOP
My love to you, to Ned, and to Pop and
many thanks to the Wheller family
STOP DULCIE
```

The premier! *Mr. Anderson must be real important,* I thought once again.

"We saw Dr. Desort, and he'll be coming to see Pop tomorrow," Mr. Anderson said. "So we'll know better about going home once we get a good report from the doctor."

"You got a letter, Jessie," Dad said, pulling a pretty green envelope out of his jacket pocket.

"It's from Sandra!" I grabbed the envelope, opened it, and read the letter quickly. "She's so nice!"

"How long has it been since you've seen her?" Ned asked.

"I've never met her, but I have her picture. I guess you'd say that she's not just a cousin—she's my friend-girl. I tell her everything in my letters—like when I'm upset. And she writes back so comforting-like."

"It's good to have a friend like that," Ned acknowledged. "Maybe she'll come to visit you someday. You could show her the sights."

"What sights? There's nothin' here to see. On the other hand there'd be lots of things for me to do if I went to visit her in Boston. Her folks are friends with two famous radio hosts that have a show called *Boston Morning*. I hear tell nearly everyone in New England listens in on their car radios as they go to work. It's real popular. Maybe I'd meet them if I went to Boston to visit Sandra."

"Well, what does she say?" Erik asked.

I glanced through the letter. "She loves to ride horseback. She wants to get her own horse. I think the horses there are bigger than ours."

"Of course they are. Ours are considered to be ponies," Erik said.

"How old is your cousin?" Ned asked.

"She's fifteen. Just a year older than me."

"More than a year," Erik said. "You won't be fourteen until July. Sandra's already fifteen."

I wanted to step on my brother's toes. Instead I ignored him. But he knew right well that I wanted Ned to think I was older. Mom said Ned was almost sixteen.

Dad and Mr. Anderson ordered coffee and doughnuts, and although Melloy McCrumb and his pal had their heads together, I could tell they were listening to us.

Ned leaned across the table and quietly told his father what happened with McCrumb: how he spoke so harshly to Clara and how he had kicked Blizzard.

"Something has got to be done, Dad," I whispered urgently. "I'm afeared for Clara."

Mr. Anderson spoke up. "As soon as I get back to St. John's, I'm going to check on their rights to Clara," he said. "There are records there, I'm sure."

"I don't know about that, Don," said Dad. "Sometimes, way out in these little ports, things aren't done in a legal way. Someone might not be able to take care of their child, and another family will show kindness and welcome the little one in as one of their own. It's done often."

"Maybe so, but there are laws about mistreatment of children—and animals, too, for that matter." Mr. Anderson spoke with authority, and I knew that he could and would do something to help Clara. And I hoped that Melloy was listening, as he seemed to be. I could see him hold up his hand to silence his friend as Mr. Anderson was speaking. Perhaps Mr.

Anderson's authority might scarify him into being wary of his conduct with Clara.

We finished our little lunch and were heading to the boat when I was surprised to see Meta, Polly, and Trudy walking by. I ran out to see them.

"Meta! Tomorrow you'll be living here in Gull Harbor for real!" I yelled as I caught up with them. "I saw the boats ready to bring your house here. It's so exciting."

Meta's face was all aglow. "Oh, Jessie, it's going to be so good to be in my own home again."

"I wish I could stay and watch your house floated in tomorrow."

Polly whispered something to her sister, and suddenly the two of them flew off in another direction. "Where are you going?" I called after them. But they didn't answer. I turned to Meta.

"Before I leave, I want to tell you about little Clara Cadigan. I gave her some clothes that came from Boston. They're like span-new. I hopes she gets to wear them. I don't trust the McCrumbs to let her have them. She looks so sad, poor little angishore."

"I'll keep an eye on her," Meta promised.

"Are you coming, Jessie?" Dad called from the boat.

"I sure wish you could stay," Meta said.

I started down the steps to the wharf, where my dad and the others were waiting, when suddenly Trudy and Polly came running up to me.

"Stay! Stay, Jessie!" Trudy called. "We asked Mom if you can stay over to watch Meta's house float back tomorrow. She said yes! So please don't leave."

"Yes, stay with us, Jessie. Stay over until Monday . . . if your dad can come back for you then," Polly begged.

"Let's ask him," I said, racing down to the boat. "Dad! Can I stay with the Doyles until Monday? Please. Just this once? They've invited me to watch Meta's house floated into shore."

Dad was taken aback, I could tell. This was one of the times when I wished we had telephones, 'cause I knew Mom would say okay. "I . . . I don't know if your mother would approve," he stammered.

"Oh, let her stay, Dad," Erik said. "Auntie Liz and Uncle Pete invited her. Besides, Jessie's been closed in all winter, with the snow and the harbor frozen. . . ."

I could have thrown my arms around my brother when he stood up for me like that. It sort of canceled some of the mean things he'd done.

"Are the Doyles related to you?" Ned asked.

"No, out here we just call grown-ups 'uncle' and 'aunt'—especially if they're people we really like."

Mr. Anderson grinned. "Then I hope you'll call *me* Uncle Don from now on."

"Okay, Uncle Don," I answered, shy-like. I turned and tugged at Dad's sleeve. "How about it, Dad? May I stay?"

"I guess it will be all right, if Auntie Liz and Uncle Pete said so," Dad agreed. "Besides, we may be bringin' the Andersons back here to take the train on Monday, so . . ."

I took in a breath. Did that mean that Ned would be leaving that soon? "Oh, I'm sorry. I forgot you might be leavin' us," I said to Uncle Don and Ned.

"Don't alarm yourself, Jessie," Uncle Don replied. "We'll see you before you go."

"So go on, now," Dad said. "We'll see you on Monday."

Meta and the Doyle twins did a little dance on the wharf, and then, all holding hands, we raced up the steps and headed to the Doyle house.

We hadn't got halfway up the road when I heard Dad yelling, "Jessie!" I turned around to see Blizzard bounding toward me with Dad following.

When they caught up with me, Dad was laughing. "I wish you had seen your dog. I couldn't get him into the boat with us. He went back and forth from the boat to the steps, all the while keeping an eye on you. He just couldn't make up his mind. So, here he is. I guess he's decided to stay with you. I hope it won't cause a problem."

Blizzard was now wagging his tail as if to say, *Jessie, I want to hang about with you.*

"Blizzard can stay!" Trudy said.

"Our folks love Blizzard," Polly added. "He can sleep on the porch."

"Well, if you're sure," Dad said as he waved good-bye.

So even though Blizzard was a boy, he stayed with us girls.

CHAPTER 11

Weekend Visit

The rest of Friday afternoon was such fun. Brianna Briggs and Margie Rand and some other girls joined in too. We jumped rope, with one girl holding each end. I couldn't play this at home by myself, so I wasn't good at group jump-roping. But I leaped in when it was my turn, and everyone sang out, "All in together, girls. A very fine weather, girls!"

I felt bad when I stepped on the rope and my group was out. But no one got mad at me, because they were so glad that I was there. Blizzard watched as he lay contentedly nearby, his head on his paws.

We were having lots of fun, when a group of boys came by to watch and tease. One boy, Mike Hawley, put his foot on the rope every time we tried to jump.

"Stop it, Mike!" Polly yelled, and chased him away, but he stuck out his tongue. He kept coming back and ruining our game, so we moved to the back of the Doyles' house and played batsy against the side of their shed. "Eenie, slapsy, twirly round the batsy," we all called, as each one of us took a turn. At first each girl had to bounce the ball off the shed while she rolled her hands like a windmill; then she'd have to catch the ball on the rebound. We were all able to do that.

The game got harder as we added touching the head, elbows, knees—and then all of those moves at one toss of the ball. Everyone did well except Brianna, who was out because the ball hit the ground before she finished. But I was able to do a double turnaround plus all the other moves and still catch the ball.

"Jessie, you're so good at this!" Polly said.

"That's because it's a game I can play by myself at home."

That night Auntie Liz Doyle made a huge dinner, with pork roast that melted in my mouth and turnips mashed up with potatoes. For dessert we had thick bread pudding loaded with figs and currants. Blizzard had a feast too, with a big bone full of marrow.

Later we girls sat on the porch and talked. I hadn't realized how much fun it would be to spend this much time with my friends. "I almost wish I could go to school just so I'd be with you all."

"Then do it, Jessie!" Meta begged.

"*Almost!*" I repeated. "I said I *almost* wished I could go to school with you."

"I'll have my own room when my house is floated in," Meta added. "You can live with my family during the school year—like I did with the Doyle family. Lots of kids do that."

"Miss Campbell will be shocking happy," Trudy said. "She thinks you're smart and should be in school."

"I tried school once when I was little," I reminded them. "But I was already reading, so Gran said it was a waste of time to go all that way."

"Oh, I'm afeared Miss Campbell ain't sharp enough to take on Jessie," Polly said, quite seriously. "You're smarter than any of us."

"It's my gran who's the smart one," I said. "She's my teacher, and she knows just about everything there is to know about anything!"

"I'm more afeared of your gran than Miss Campbell," Meta said, rolling her eyes. "Your gran is quite scary, let me tell."

"Miss Campbell is nice. She'd lend a hand to anyone who needed help," Trudy said. "When Clara doesn't bring lunch, Miss Campbell shares hers with Clara."

"Does that happen often? Doesn't Clara have a lunch every day?" I asked.

"No, not every day," Trudy said. "I give her some of mine when she has none."

"Me too," Meta said. "Don't worry, Jessie. We're all watching over her."

I hoped so. Blizzard lay at my feet, and I ran my fingers through his fur and tried to let go of the bad feelings I had about the McCrumb family.

That night I shared a bedroom with Meta. Trudy, Polly, Meta, and I brushed each other's hair, and Meta put mine in a ponytail like we had seen in a movie star magazine Sandra had sent me in the clothes barrel.

"Your hair is so long and beautiful, Jessie. It comes all the way to your waist," Polly said.

"The color is the same as your grandmother's," Meta added.

Trudy leaned closer to me. "How does she keep it so black . . . and so shiny?"

I put my finger to my lips. "Promise not to tell?" The three girls nodded. "I've seen her rinsing her hair with . . ." I paused, then whispered, "sugar and water."

"Oh, morrow yah," Meta said with a gasp. "I don't believe a word of it!" But then she whispered, "Shall we try it?" Before I could answer, she was flying down-stairs. When she returned she was carrying a bowl. "Here it is. Water and sugar. This will be fun!"

I took my ponytail out and then we took turns dragging a big ivory comb into the water and then through each other's hair.

Before long our hair was drying—and very sticky. "I'm sleepy," Meta said.

"Me too," Trudy and Polly said together. The twins left for bed, still drying their hair with towels.

"See you in the morning," I called after them.

"Do you think my hair will shine in the sun tomorrow?" Meta asked.

"Gran's always shines," I replied.

Meta and I talked a lot, and before we went to sleep, Auntie Liz came in and gave me a flashlight, in case I needed to get up during the night.

Gradually Meta became quiet and her breathing even and I knew she was asleep. I lay there thinking about tomorrow and Meta's house being floated into Gull Harbor. It would be fun to watch. At the same time I knew there was sadness for many folks who'd had to leave their homes. My grandparents had lived out on Lonesome Island years ago, but they were never lonesome. And although they were poor, they didn't want for anything. Grandpa fished. Gran worked in their garden and knitted beautiful things with the wool from their own sheep. They had cows for milking. And they were all happy. Except . . . when the storm came—and caused the shipwreck when my grandfather and my uncles were returning from a trip.

When Grandpa and the others died in that awful storm, Gran sold the animals and then moved to our house on the mainland. Later, Dad crossed over to Lonesome Isle and brought back her special belongings, like the teapot that had been passed down to Gran—and other things. Dad had gone out there many times to check on the place. Since then the house had fallen apart out there, but the huge barn was still strong and standing.

As I brooded over all this, I could hear Uncle Pete and Auntie Liz's voices from the kitchen.

"Once the Rideouts get their house over here tomorrow, we'll all be in for the money the government will send us for moving," Uncle Pete was saying.

I knew that the government didn't pay folks for resettlement until everyone on the island or in the outport had left.

"The Rideouts held out for quite a while, but they knew the pressure was on from the rest of us who left Stepping Stone Island," Uncle Pete went on.

"I wonder how much we'll get?" Auntie Liz asked. "Especially since we moved out earlier."

"It could be anywhere from fifty dollars to three or four hundred," Uncle Pete answered.

"Fifty dollars wouldn't be enough. If that's all we get, I wish we'd stayed where we were. It was nice with our gardens and our own flakes for drying the fish."

"It's good for the children to go to school and see other kids," Uncle Pete argued. "And we can still fish...."

Auntie Liz said something, but her voice was low, and it was hard to hear. I was drifting off to the low murmur of their voices when I heard the name McCrumb and something about the horses. I became awake again and strained to listen, but I couldn't make it out.

Then I thought about the horses out there on Stepping Stone Island. What would become of them? After working hard for so many years, towing heavy loads of wood, in the winter pulling sleighs and in the springtime barrels of kelp from the shore for fertilizer ... after all their help over hundreds of years, would they now be forgotten, deserted, and starving?

I turned over on my side and could hear Meta's soft breathing. I fluffed my pillow and tried to sleep, but soon my thoughts drifted to Clara. Was she hungry tonight? Did the McCrumbs ever show her affection and care? Or was she discarded and afraid, like the abandoned ponies on Stepping Stone Island?

CHAPTER 12

Tragedy Strikes!

It seemed I'd only been asleep a short while when the morning light crept through the window and Meta began to stir.

She blinked at me with sleepy eyes and yawned. "What time is it? They're going to start floating the house back at seven o'clock."

I strained to see the little clock on the table. "It's six thirty."

She sat up and almost jumped out of the bed. "Let's go. Come on!" She was out of her pajamas and into her clothes in a flash. "I can smell coffee and bacon. The Doyles are already up." Her voice was muffled as she pulled on a sweatshirt. "Let's go. Quick!" I could hear her bare feet slapping as she dashed down the stairs.

I dressed quickly and combed my hair. It was sticky, and I could hardly draw a comb through it. Finally I plaited it in one big braid and then went to the kitchen, where Auntie Liz had made scrambled eggs, bacon, and bangbellies. The smell was scrumptious. Uncle

Pete had gone down to watch the house come in, and the twins had already eaten. Blizzard, who had slept on the porch, was pawing at the door. "Here's more leftovers for the dog," said Trudy, handing me a dish.

Outside, the air was fresh and clean, with the scent of the sea and fish on the wind. "Here you go, boy." I set the food on the floor, and Blizzard's big nose disappeared into the bowl as his tail wagged happily.

I could hear the sound of engines coming from the water and could see the smoke from the tugboats. They were on their way to Stepping Stone to navigate the Rideouts' house to shore. A graded ramp that had been scraped out by the shore, and a bulldozer was down there waiting to bring the house onto the new foundation.

"They're heading out to the island," I announced as I went back inside and sat down to the breakfast set out for me.

Meta jumped up from the table, but Auntie Liz put her hand up. "Just sit and eat. There's plenty of time to watch the action."

Meta gulped down her breakfast while the twins waited impatiently by the door. But I was still tired from not sleeping, and I moved more slowly than the others. "I'm not through yet," I said with a yawn. "Shouldn't we help with the dishes?"

"Don't mind the dishes," Auntie Liz said. "You can all help out by 'n' by."

I gulched my apple juice and followed the girls, who were already starting up the road. Blizzard barked and bounded after me.

Down at the shore a crowd stood with Meta's parents—the Rideouts—and watched as the boats tugged at the cables attached to the house. At the end of the pier, Aunt Annie clung to Uncle George as their house moved slowly away from the island and toward the mainland.

"She's on her way!" someone yelled.

"What a sight! I gets a kick out of watchin' 'em. Those clumsy houses weren't made for floatin' on the water," Uncle George said, chuckling.

"It's tipping, Dad!" Meta yelled, dashing down the stairs to join her parents.

"It's only because of the boats' wakes," I called as I followed her onto the pier.

Suddenly Mike Hawley raced in front of me full speed. "Get outta my way!" he yelled as he smashed into me.

"Ow!" I tripped and fell onto the rough, splintery boards of the wharf. "You wild little bullamarue!" I screamed after him.

He ducked behind a group of men, and peering out he stuck his tongue out at me. "You can't catch me, Jessie Wheller," he taunted.

Even with my bleeding hands and knees, I went after him and grabbed him by the shirt. He wiggled and squirmed, and I would have clouted him, but at that moment the splinters in the palms of my hands felt like tiny knives and hurt so much I had to let him go. It was hard not to cry, especially when Blizzard whined sympathetically and lapped my face.

Aunt Annie ran to me. "Are you all right, Jessie?"

I pointed to my knees, where blood had soaked my pants. When Uncle George came over and took my hands to pull me up, I gasped in more pain. "Oh, maid," he said, looking at my palms. "You tried to break your fall, and now you're all splintered and bloody."

"You poor thing," Meta said. "You should go back to the Doyles' house, Jessie. You've been hurt bad!"

"And where is that chucklehead?" Uncle George exclaimed, looking around. "Ah, there he is. I should have known. It's Jack Hawley's kid." He started toward the boy, who had now croodled down behind a barrel. "Get over here, Mike. Over here now!" Uncle George yelled. "I'm takin' you up to your father, who ought to paddle you for bein' such a trouble-maker."

Mike ignored Uncle George; he was more interested in tormenting me. "Come and get me, Jessie Wheller!" Mike made a face at me and ducked behind a barrel.

Despite my pain I lurched toward the huge cask where he had hidden.

Toooot! I looked up to see a large boat heading into the dock. Once the passengers came off the boat, the wharf would be even more crowded. *Never mind chasing Mike,* I thought. *I just want to get away from all these people and go back to the Doyles' house.* But at that moment Mike ran out, darted away from between Uncle George and me, and then wound through the groups of spectators on the wharf.

"Get over here, Mike!" another man yelled. "You won't get away this time, you half-wit!"

Once again the boy stuck out his tongue, laughed, then wee-geed in and out as hands reached out to catch him at the end of the pier. He raced in the direction of a stack of barrels waiting to be shipped, near one edge of the wharf.

By now I was hurting too much to care whether they caught Mike or not. I headed painfully toward the stairs with Blizzard by my side. Then I heard folks yelling.

"Watch out, Mike!"

"Get out of there!"

"Oh, my blessed Lord! He's sure to fall into the path of that boat!"

I turned to see Mike Hawley jumping from one barrel to another, balancing himself unsteadily as he tried to get away from the hands that reached out to grab him. Suddenly he tottered, then for a moment seemed to regain his footing. I watched in horror as he wobbled, lost his balance, and fell off the wharf into the deep water.

The steamer honked over and over. We could tell the captain was trying to reverse direction as the motor roared and churned waves. But it was too late to maneuver the ship into reverse. It was still on a path heading directly for Mike Hawley.

"Oh, dear Lord!" Aunt Annie screamed. "He'll drown!"

"Get him out!" someone yelled. "Throw him a line!"

"It's too late; he's done for."

Mike surfaced from the water, his eyes large in fear as he saw the ship bearing down on him.

And then he was gone.

CHAPTER 13

Blame

S ave him! Save him!" cried Mike's mother, who had been up on the road watching the events.

"Oh, it's too late," someone murmured. "The poor lad."

"Get these barrels out of the way. We've got to look for him," Uncle Pete exclaimed.

He and Uncle George pulled the barrels aside. They stared into the water, which was now turning a dark red near the spot where Mike had gone down.

I stood as if frozen, my heart pounding and my stomach ready to heave. By now the steamer had moved into reverse and was backing away slowly from the wharf.

"There he is!" Mrs. Hawley screamed, pushing her way down the steps. "I can see him. There!" She pointed to a limp form just under the surface of the water. "Get him out, someone!" she begged.

Uncle George found a boat hook, then climbed into a rowboat and looked for oars. But there were none. By now Blizzard had nudged his way to the edge of the wharf.

"Somebody get Mike!" Mrs. Hawley screamed again.

Instantly, as if her words were a command, Blizzard leaped from the wharf into the churning water. Several people cheered, "Get him, Blizzard! Go get that boy!"

Blizzard swam quickly toward the dark-haired form in the water. When he reached Mike, he swam around for a moment, as if deciding where to take hold of him.

"Bring him in, Blizzard!" I called.

Several men climbed down to the shoreline next to the wharf, where the water was shallow.

"Aye, bring him in, boy!" they called. "Good dog!"

Blizzard gently grabbed the back of Mike's plaid shirt with his teeth and began tugging him toward the rocky shoreline.

Mrs. Hawley jumped down off the wharf, falling to her knees on the stones. Then she got up and stumbled to her son. "Oh, my boy, my boy!"

My own eyes filled as I watched her sob and cry.

Blizzard reached the shore, dragging Mike's body. Uncle George and the others waded into the water, then tenderly lifted Mike up in their arms.

"Mike! Mike!" Mrs. Hawley cried over and over. "Speak to me, boy."

Blizzard climbed up the rocks and onto the dock, looking around for me.

"Over here, Blizzard," I said, throwing my arms around his neck. "Good boy. You brave, wonderful dog." His wet tail wagged and sprayed water over me.

"How lucky your dog was here," Polly said to me. "No one could have rescued Mike as quickly as Blizzard."

"You're a right good dog, Blizzard," Trudy agreed.

Blizzard's tail swished again, and he licked Trudy's hand.

But our attention went quickly back to the shoreline, and we shoved our way through the crowd lining the side of the dock, with Blizzard next to us. Below, the men had taken off their coats and jackets and made a soft spot, where they placed Mike.

"Is he dead?" Meta whispered to me,

"I don't know, but look how white his face is." Suddenly I heard loud cries from the road. "What's happened to my boy?" Jack Hawley flew down the steps three at a time, evidently having just heard about the accident. With him was Melloy McCrumb.

"Get out of the way!" Melloy shouted, pushing people aside.

They both leaped onto the stony beach. "Oh, my blessed Lord!" Jack yelled when he saw the pale boy lying still in a pool of blood.

"How did this happen?" Melloy asked, looking around at the crowd.

"He's still alive, Jack," Uncle Pete called out to Mike's father. "But someone go and get Dr. Desort the once!"

"He's on his way," came the answer from the onlookers.

"Mike's alive!" The words were repeated over and over among the crowd.

Mrs. Hawley unbuttoned Mike's shirt and carefully pulled it off, revealing his torn and bloody arms. She gasped at the sight of her son's injuries. "Where's Dr. Desort?" she screamed.

At that very moment the doctor came running down the steps, carrying his black bag, followed by two men with a stretcher. They climbed down to the shoreline where Mike lay.

Jack Hawley pulled his hysterical wife away from their son and made room for the doctor. Melloy seemed to take over, as he shoved people aside and stood close to the boy, his arms crossed.

"Save Mike. Please save him," Mrs. Hawley begged, looking back at the still body of her son. "Save my boy."

Dr. Desort got down on his knees, examined Mike's arms, and then opened his bag. He took out what looked like a large elastic band and tied it tightly around Mike's right arm, above the elbow. The blood that had been spurting out of the torn skin now slowed almost to a stop. The doctor checked Mike's left arm, shook his head, and wrapped the injury in white gauze bandages.

The doctor then cut off Mike's trousers with a knife and examined his legs. "Mike, can you hear us, lad?" the doctor asked loudly. But there was no response.

Dr. Desort stood up and signaled for the men to lift Mike onto the stretcher. "Take him to my office for now," he called out. "He needs immediate surgery. I doubt if he could make it to the hospital in his condition."

The men carefully lifted Mike onto the stretcher, and with help from others they were able to bring

Mike to the wharf, up the stairs, and then to the road. Faith and Jack Hawley tearfully walked beside their son as he was carried to Dr. Desort's office. Melloy McCrumb marched in front of the procession, waving aside anyone in their way.

The folks on the dock spoke to one another in hushed voices about the horrible accident.

The ship that had gone over Mike was finally docked, and the captain came out. "How's that boy?" he asked anxiously.

"He's alive, thanks to that dog over there," one of his crew answered, pointing to Blizzard.

"Aye, the boy would have drowned for certain if Blizzard hadn't brought him in so quickly," Uncle George said.

Hearing the word "dog," Blizzard perked up his ears, and the captain bent down and patted my dog's head. "Good work, Blizzard," he said. Blizzard licked the captain's face with his slobbery tongue, and a few people laughed. The captain stood up and wiped his face with a handkerchief. "There was nothing I could do to prevent the boat from hitting that kid. He should have never been prancin' around on those barrels. What on earth was he doin'?"

"He was tormentin' one of the girls," Uncle George explained, "teasin' and knockin' her over."

"Oh, the boy is a handful," Uncle Pete said. "But by the same token we'll all be prayin' for him."

"Why is there such a crowd down here today?" the captain asked.

"We're watchin' my house bein' towed to shore." Uncle George gestured to the house, which was now more than halfway to the mainland.

"Mike's accident was a right awful thing," Meta's mother said. She took a look at my bloody pants and splintered hands. "But Mike sure is a bullamarue."

"Blizzard is our hero," Auntie Liz said, patting my dog's big head. "And he gets an extra big juicy bone tonight, let me tell!" At the word "bone" Blizzard whined, and his whole body wiggled.

The twins walked me back to their home, while Blizzard trotted along with us. Meta stayed with her parents to watch their house come in.

"You're limping," Trudy said. "You must hurt really bad."

"My knees smert and feel all messy with blood," I said. "But they don't hurt as much as my hands with all these splinters." I held up my palms for her to see.

"My mom will fix you up, Jessie." Polly put her arm around my shoulders.

On our way back to the Doyles' house flickering shadows fell over us. We looked up to see three crows overhead. "Oh, no!" Trudy cried as they fluttered to the bare limbs of a nearby tree.

"One for wet, two for dry; three for sorrow, four to die," Polly recited. "Do you suppose this is a sign that Mike is goin' to die?"

"There are only three," Trudy said. "Don't look up. We don't want to see another."

"Stop it!" I yelled. "That's a lot of pishogue!"

"No, it's not," said Polly.

"Three is for sorrow," her sister insisted.

"That's 'cause you're Irish," I said. "My family is Scottish, and we say three crows are for marriage and four are for birth. Besides, no one believes that stuff anymore."

The twins looked at each other. "We do," they said together. "And the Irish are right."

I didn't want to argue about crows, and I didn't want my friends to be mad at me, so I said nothing more. But deep inside I was worried too, and I didn't look up, for fear of seeing another crow.

When we got back to the Doyles', the twins left me with their mom and returned to watch the Rideouts' house, which probably was being set on the foundation by now.

I sat at the kitchen table while Auntie Liz removed the long splinters from my palms and fingers. She washed each of my cuts and bruises and then coated them with stinging iodine. I tried hard not to cry, but tears trickled down my cheeks. Auntie Liz wiped them with her apron. "It's almost lunchtime, Jessie," she said gently. "I'll heat up some beef stew for you, and then I want you to go up and take a nap."

I slept soundly for a few hours and was awakened by loud voices coming from down in the house. Was that my name being tossed about? I climbed out of bed and tiptoed to the stairway.

"So, how is Mike, anyway?" Auntie Liz asked.

"After Doc fixed him up as well as he could, they took him to the hospital. Faith's gone with him. She's out of her mind with worry. If it weren't for that Wheller girl, my son would not be badly hurt and taken to the hospital. And you're keepin' her here. I wants to see that girl right now."

"How did you know Jessie is here?"

"That big black and white dog of hers is sittin' right out there on your porch."

What does he think I did to Mike, that he's blaming me?

"Jessie's sleepin', Jack. Your son was running wild and knocked her over. You should see the cuts and scrapes—," Auntie Liz began.

"Cuts and scrapes! My boy was pushed right into the water and nearly drowned...not to mention the injuries to his arms and legs from the steamer! He'll never be the same, and I'm holdin' that Wheller girl responsible."

"That's a lot of balderdash. He wasn't pushed. Jessie didn't lay a hand on him," Auntie Liz insisted.

"He was runnin' away from her," Jack Hawley said. "I heard it from someone who saw the whole thing."

"Don't believe one word of it, Jack. I was there, and I saw the whole thing too. You should be grateful that Mike's alive. It was Jessie's dog that saved his life," came Auntie Liz's response. "I'm sorry to say it, especially with Mike hurt and in the hospital, but face it: Your son is a troublemaker. And what happened, sad as it is, might teach him a lesson not to run about knocking people over."

"Mike don't mean to cause trouble." Jack Hawley paused, and I could hear him blow his nose. "Besides," he went on tearfully, "you should see my boy. No kid should ever be hurt like that. The doctor doesn't think he'll ever have the use of his right arm. How can he make a livin' when he grows up? How can he fish or—"

"You need to calm down, Jack," Auntie Liz interrupted gently. "Come on, now, sit down and have a cup of tea with me. You'll feel better if you do."

"Nothin's goin' to make me feel better until my boy's back home and well. It might be weeks before he can come home from the hospital. And how am I supposed to pay for those expenses? Walt Wheller's goin' to hear from me, let me tell."

I tiptoed back into the bedroom, climbed into bed, and pulled the pillow over my ears. I didn't want to hear any more. But I couldn't turn off the voices in my own head.

What if Mike loses his arm? He couldn't fish or do much with one arm. He looked so white lying there on the ground. And . . . all that blood. Was it really my fault? He did start it, though, chasing me and teasing and banging into me. If they blame me, I'll tell everyone that he was the one who started it.

But maybe it doesn't matter who starts something like that. I chased after him, didn't I? That probably egged him on. Maybe if I'd ignored him, he'd have stopped pestering me.

So maybe it is my fault after all.

CHAPTER 14

Where Is Clara?

I stayed in bed the rest of the day, and at suppertime the twins brought me soup and Irish soda bread and tried to make me feel better. I didn't want to stay one more day in Gull Harbor. All I could think of was how I could get home.

Polly, Trudy, and Auntie Liz invited me to go to church with them tomorrow—Sunday morning—as the priest was going to pray for Mike Hawley. The Doyles were Catholic, but I wasn't.

"I'm hurting too badly to go. Thank you, though," I said. "I'll pray for Mike. I don't want him to die, and I don't want him to be handicapped, either."

"It's all right, Jessie," Auntie Liz said. "You can stay here tomorrow while we go to church. I'll tell anyone who asks that you're in bed with your injuries. They know that you were hurt too. Try not to worry, child. Everyone who was there knows it wasn't your fault."

That night I curled up and half slept, planning what I would do in the morning. *When everyone is in church,*

I'll walk home, I decided. *I'll leave a note so the Doyles won't worry. The path to the Cliffs is only about five or six miles. Blizzard will be with me, and even though the woods this time of year are damp and full of muck, we'll be okay,* I told myself.

I wished I could have seen Clara while I was here, but she'd never showed up, even during all the excitement about Meta's house and Mike's accident. Was she all right? Why hadn't she joined everyone on the waterfront today? I rolled over and moaned at the pain in my knees. My sore hands clasped the cool pillow, and I finally fell asleep.

Sunday morning was bright and warm with the feeling that spring had really come. Then I remembered the terrible accident on the wharf yesterday, and I felt sad and scared. *How is Mike today?* I wondered. Jack Hawley's words rang over and over in my head: "I'm holdin' that Wheller girl responsible."

The twins were already up and dressed. Meta had spent the night on a cot in her old house, and I was sure she was only too happy to be home again, even though everything inside the house must be topsy-turvy.

I could hear the Doyle family in the kitchen and

the sounds of clinking pans; I could smell the coffee. I joined them downstairs. I was eager to get on the fairy path, as the old, seldom-used trail was called, and head back home. But of course I wouldn't tell the Doyles I was leaving. They'd beg me to stay until Monday morning, when my dad would come for me.

"Here's Jessie," Auntie Liz said. "How are you today, maid?"

"I'm very well, considerin'," I answered, serving myself a large portion of bangbellies and bacon. I'd need a good start for my long walk back home.

"Good girl, Jessie," Uncle Pete said with a smile. "I can see your hands are better and you're hungry."

"Aye, don't make shy, maid. Eat up," Auntie Liz said. "After your fall yesterday I'm certain you're still hurting. Let me see your knees." I pulled up the pajamas that the girls had lent me, and Auntie Liz took a look and examined the cuts. "I'll put new bandages on them today," she said.

"My hands feel better," I told her.

The family was all dressed and ready to head to the church down the road. "Will you be all right here alone?" Trudy asked.

"I'll just sit here by the window and watch the folks

go by until you come back. Say a prayer for Mike Hawley for me."

"We will, Jessie," Polly promised.

"We've already fed Blizzard. He's out on the back porch as happy as a clam in a mudflat," Trudy said with a laugh.

Sunday mornings everyone walked to church, and I was curious to see just who would be going. Would Clara be going to church with the McCrumbs? I couldn't help feeling that all was not well with her.

After the Doyles left, I sat by the window, wondering just how I'd go about my long walk back to the Cliffs. I didn't feel well. I was hurt, and I was also sad that Mike was so badly injured.

Outside, families were heading for church. I saw Brianna Briggs and Margie Rand, hand in hand in their Sunday best, trailing along behind their families. Other people I didn't know marched past, their prayer books in their hands.

I took in a breath as Melloy McCrumb and his wife walked by, dressed in Sunday-go-to-meeting clothes. With them were Jack and Faith Hawley, arm in arm. Folks were pausing to give sympathy and show concern for Mike.

Oh, I had to get home! I knew the way along the path that led to the Cliffs. Erik and I had walked it several times just for the fun of it, while Dad came by boat. I was sure I'd never get lost. I stood up to get ready for my long walk, when I saw a little girl in a familiar coat and bonnet. *My coat—the one I gave to Clara!* A feeling of relief flooded over me. Then I looked more closely. It wasn't Clara! The girl in my coat and hat was a stranger!

So! The McCrumbs never gave my gifts to Clara. They probably sold them and kept the money. But where is Clara?

I was ready to leave. I searched for a piece of paper and pencil. Then I wrote a note to the Doyle family and left it on the table:

> *Thank you so much for having me this weekend. I've decided to walk home. It's not too far, and I have Blizzard with me. I'll be back to see you soon. Love, Jessie.*

I quickly changed into my own clothes. My hands were still sore, but I tried not to think about them. I was worried about Clara. Her foster parents had gone to church without her, so maybe she was home alone. I just *had* to see her before I left.

When I went outside, Blizzard was sleeping on the porch. "Get up, boy. Let's go see Clara, and then we're going home."

I headed toward the McCrumb house. The town was quiet because everyone was at church. I tiptoed to the front door and knocked. "Clara!" I called. But there was no answer. Where was she? I knocked again and waited, but no one came to the door, so I decided to go on my way. As we went down the walkway from the house to the road, I passed their barn. Suddenly Blizzard stopped, listening. Then he barked.

Was there a horse in the barn? Had the McCrumbs brought their horse back from Stepping Stone Island? I expected to hear a whinny or a snort. "Come on, Blizzard," I called. "Let's get going. Church will be out soon. I want to leave before then."

Blizzard ignored me and headed for the big barn door, where he barked again. Then he scratched at the door and whined.

"What's wrong, boy?" When I approached the barn, I thought I heard something—a cry? Clara?

I knocked on the door. "Clara! Are you there?"

There was no answer, but I could hear sobbing. "Clara! Is that you? It's me, Jessie."

"Jessie! Please help me. Please, Jessie."

I lifted the large slat of wood that fastened the door. "I'm coming, Clara." The door opened. Clara was sitting on the dirt floor, crying. As the bright sunlight burst into the darkness of the barn, I could see welts on her face and bare legs.

"Oh, Jessie. They punished me and then locked me in here. I've been locked in here for two days! Please help me. I don't want to live here anymore. Help me, Jessie." She put her hands over her face and sobbed.

I was sure my own heart was breaking as I gathered her into my arms. "Oh, I will help you, Clara," I promised. "You're comin' home with me right now!"

CHAPTER 15

The Fairy Horse

"Come on, Clara," I said, pulling her by the hand. "Let's leave now before church gets out."

"What if they find me?" A worried frown creased Clara's forehead. "They'll beat me again. I know they will."

"They won't know where you are. You'll be safe at our house. Hurry." I looked at her raggedy dress. "They left you out here without a coat?"

"I had a horse blanket to wrap around me."

"You'll need a sweater or something warm."

"Inside," she said. "I'll get it." She headed for the rear of the house. "The back door is never locked."

I waited at the door nervously. How long did the church service take? I wondered. "Hurry, Clara," I called. "We've got to leave now." When she came out she was shoving her arms into the ugly coat.

"They didn't let you have the nice coat I left you, did they?"

"No. I felt so bad, Jessie. I begged them if I could

just keep the hat, and that's when Ma slapped me."

I could see tears forming again. "Don't think about it anymore," I said gently. "You'll come stay with us. My dad will never let them take you away—not when he hears about all this. Come on!" Blizzard jumped off the steps, his tail wagging, ready to go.

The church was down the road to the left, past the Doyles' house. We went to the right, which led to a meadow and then the woods beyond. I hoped no one was around to notice us. We ran up the road and through the field, which was marshy and wet. As we passed through the field, I noticed that a section had been fenced off recently. The new wood had not been treated and still had the whiteness and scent of fresh lumber. Inside the enclosure four horses were grazing.

"Who built that fence?" I muttered. "And whose horses are those?"

"Pa and Jack Hawley built it. One of the horses is Pa's. He brought him over from the island." Clara was quiet for a moment. "Hmm, I thought there were five horses there. But there are only four."

"Where did the other horses come from?"

"They came from one of the islands—maybe

Stepping Stone. Or Pebble Rock. They're tellin' everyone they rescued them."

I was surprised. "Since when do they care about the horses?"

"Pa and Jack were sitting at the table one night talkin' about the horses—that they're goin' to get them together and fence them in. Then . . . he said somethin' about . . . I can't remember."

I knew there had to be a reason for those two men to be concerned about the horses. They were cruel to animals. Hadn't Melloy McCrumb kicked Blizzard? *How come they're rescuing the horses? There must be some other reason.* Well, I couldn't figure it out right then. We had to get away as fast as we could.

We had reached the edge of the woods. "There's the beginning of the fairy path," I said, pointing to a small opening in the brush. It was hardly visible. We ducked onto the dim trail. Clara clung to me as we walked on the uneven pathway. Blizzard trotted ahead of us, and in the darkness of the woods the white fur on his coat was like a guiding light.

"Now tell me what happened. Why did your folks lock you in the barn for two days?"

Clara stopped walking and looked up at me. Her big brown eyes looked huge against her pale face in the gloom of the woods. "I was supposed to wash and dry the dishes," she said. "But I felt real bad after supper. I told them I was sick, but Ma said, 'Don't give me excuses. Get in there and do the dishes.'"

"I went outside to bring water into the house from the well. But when I was out there, I yucked up everything. I felt dizzy and lay down on the ground—just for a minute until I felt better." Clara put her hand to her mouth. "Oh, I don't even want to remember."

"It's all right. You're safe now," I told her.

"Pa came and asked what was going on, and when he saw I was lying down, he smacked me in the face real hard. Ma yelled out the door, 'Don't hit her face. It'll show.' So I filled the pail and went back inside. I put the pail on the stove, and while I waited for the water to heat, I sat at the table and put my head on my arms. My face hurt from where he clobbered me. But for a little while I must have fallen asleep again. That's when Pa came in and found me. He made me sit on the table and take off my stockings, and he thrashed my bare legs with his belt."

I bent down and put my arms around her. "I don't

know what we'll do, Clara, but I promise you'll never go back there."

"Even if they come to get me?"

"Even if I have to hide you. I won't let them take you away."

"Thank you, Jessie," Clara said.

"Come on," I said, taking her hand. "Blizzard is waiting for us."

We walked along the winding path without speaking for a long while. The tuckamore and bushes were still bare, and the fir trees hid the sunlight from the trail. The low-lying areas were wet, sometimes up to our ankles in muck, but we just kept on. I could see that Clara was tired, but she never complained. *What a sweet, brave little girl*, I thought. No one probably knew just what she had gone through, living with the McCrumb family.

I was becoming more nervous thinking what might happen when they found her gone. Had I acted too quickly? Perhaps I should have taken her to the Doyles and let them help her. Still, no one in the Harbor had reached out to help Clara, had they? Didn't they suspect what was happening?

"Did you tell anyone that the McCrumbs were

mistreating you?" I asked. "Your teacher, or the Doyles, or . . . anyone at all?"

"Miss Campbell wondered when I didn't bring lunch sometimes. But Ma is always friendly and sweet to everyone. I don't think anyone would believe she's unkind. Besides, if I told anyone, I'd be punished." A crow cawed, and its large wings fluttered above the tree-tops. "Why do you call this the fairy path?" she asked.

"People say that paths like these, that are hardly ever used and yet seem to stay open, are cleared by the fairies for their use. See how this one is still vis-ible so we can make it out and follow it? Maybe we'll meet some fairies along the way," I said.

A little later Clara paused again. "What's a crimbil, Jessie? I know it has something to do with fairies."

"A crimbil is a changeling," I explained. "Fairies and elves are said to come in the night and exchange a fairy child for a mortal. Usually changelings are trouble-makers or are sickly."

We began walking again, and for a while Clara didn't speak. Then she paused again and said, "Ma and Pa called me a crimbil."

"Well, if you were a crimbil, I'm sure the fairies would want you back, because you are so beautiful and good."

"Maybe *you're* a fairy, Jessie, and you've come to take me back."

"Maybe I am," I said.

As we walked farther into the woods, I pointed to a hill that blocked out the noonday sun. "See that hill? Just beyond it is our house. We're almost home, Clara." Then I heard the sound of rushing water, and in a moment we rounded a bend and came to a wild brook.

"We'll have to cross the brook somehow." I couldn't help sounding concerned, and I noticed Clara's face became clouded.

"I don't want to cross. . . . The brook is angry."

"Angry?" I asked. "No, it's just the melting snow rushing away so spring can come. We'll get across. You'll see."

Blizzard, who had darted ahead, was already by the edge of the stream and lapping up the water eagerly. Suddenly he looked up and barked. I followed his gaze, and farther down the stream, among the shadows and foggy sun that filtered through the trees, I glimpsed the dark form of a horse.

Clara saw it too and grabbed my arm. "Oh, Jessie! Look! Surely that's an each-uisge. A water-horse! It's a bad sign, Jessie."

"What do you mean, a bad sign? What are you talking about? It's just a horse."

At that moment the horse tossed its head, turned, and then disappeared among the trees. For a moment I felt a chill. Where had the horse come from? And had we really seen it, or had we imagined it? Then I suddenly recalled the fairy tales Gran used to tell me—about the water-horse!

Clara covered her face with her hands. "We've got to hide. I'm afeared. Perhaps I did the wrong thing by leaving home."

"No, you did not! You had to get away to be safe."

"I'm afraid to cross the creek," Clara said. "Ma told me that water-horses are bad. They want to lead children out into the deep water. We'll drown!"

"She was telling you fairy tales, Clara. Pishogue!" I answered. "The brook isn't very deep. But it's freezing cold, I'm sure." I walked along the bank, looking for a way to get to the opposite shore. "There are some rocks up there," I said, pointing to a line of boulders. "It should be easy to jump from stone to stone and get across to the other side."

"It looks slippery, though, Jessie." Clara's voice shook fearfully as we approached the ford.

"I'll help you," I promised. "We'll jump together."

This was the first time Clara had complained during our trek through the woods, but there was no other way that I could see to get across the brook. "We're almost home. Once we cross and climb over the hill, you'll see our house and barn. Mom will have a fire going in the stove, and she'll bundle you up nice and cozy." Clara nodded and took my hand. "Come on, Blizzard," I called. "You go first."

Blizzard, who had followed us to the crossing place, looked up at me uncertainly. "It's okay, Blizzard," I said, clapping my hands and pointing to the frothing, bubbling water. "Go on. Go home, boy!" Blizzard stepped into the frothing waves, backed out, and once again gave me a questioning look.

"See? Blizzard won't go across," Clara said. "He knows that horse was an each-uisge. He knows he'll be pulled into the water. I don't want to cross. I'm afeared, Jessie."

"We'll be all right," I insisted. But part of me was ascared, too. The current was strong, but if we could stay on the rocks, we'd be all right.

One of the boulders nearest the shore wasn't far away. I knew I could wade out, or even jump.

"Watch me," I said, and I leaped across the gushing water to the boulder. I slid and fell onto the rock, skinning my knee again, but I pulled myself up and called to Blizzard. "Come on, boy. Show Clara we can do it."

But Blizzard wouldn't move from Clara's side. "Blizzard saw the each-uisge. He knows he'll be drowned!" she called. "Jessie, come back."

So I leaped back to the shore where she and my dog waited. "All that rigmarole Henrietta McCrumb told you about the horse is nothing but pishogue," I said. "That was probably the horse that was missing from the corral. It wasn't a ghostly thing waiting to drown us." I took Clara's hand and tugged her to the water's edge. "Now, we'll go together. We'll be fine, and we'll be home soon."

Clara pulled back, but soon I had pulled her to my side. "Come on, now. One, two, three!"

We jumped safely to the first boulder without even slipping. "Good!" I said. "Now we'll go for the next one. Still holding her hand I said, "One, two, three!" and we jumped again. But this time we both slid on the rock, which was covered with moss and slimy green stuff. "Are you all right?" I asked her.

Tears were slipping down her face. "Yes, Jessie. But I'm ascared."

Suddenly a large wave came and splashed over the boulder. Clara tried to reach out to me, but she slipped and fell into the surging water.

"Oh, no!" I screamed. "I'll get you, Clara!" I said, jumping into the water after her. She cried out, and I could see her slipping under the torrent, her blond hair floating above her, then disappearing into the froth.

"Clara! Clara!" I yelled, as the raging current pulled me downstream after her. I tried to see where she was, but she had vanished in the wild water.

CHAPTER 16

Safe at the Cliffs

I gasped for breath as I bobbed in and out of the frothing rapids. My feet hit against a boulder, and I was able to grab hold of the edge. "Clara! Clara! Where are you?" I pulled myself onto the rock and stood up, knee-deep in water. I scanned the surging torrent and could see Clara struggling as the current pulled her farther downstream.

What had I done? Had I brought her away from the McCrumbs only to have her drown? Suddenly Blizzard barked and ran down along the edge of the stream, his eyes focused on Clara.

"Get her, boy. Go get Clara!" I watched hopefully as he splashed into the brook, his strong legs carrying him along with the waves. Then he turned, and I saw that he had Clara in tow, his teeth grasping her coat. "Oh, good boy, Blizzard!"

My dog pulled Clara to the opposite shore, where she was able to drag herself out of the water. Blizzard nudged her up onto the bank with his nose.

"I'm coming!" I took a leap to another boulder, then another, until I was able to wade up onto the other side.

"Clara! Are you hurt?" I ran to her and threw my arms around her. Her body shook with sobs.

"Oh, Jessie," she cried. "I was like to drown when Blizzard grabbed ahold of me." She was bivvering and her teeth chattered; her legs were bleeding from scraping the rocks, and her dripping hair clung to her cheeks.

"I'm so sorry you fell in. I promise we'll be home soon. My house is just a little way over the hill. Can you walk?"

"My legs hurt, and I'm freezing, Jessie," she moaned.

"I know. My knees are stinging too. I can go get help, if you want to wait here," I suggested.

"No! Don't leave me," Clara begged. "The each-uisge will come for me. I told you that wasn't a real horse. If it hadn't been for Blizzard, it would have pulled me under."

Blizzard shook himself several times, scattering water everywhere. Then he headed up the hill, where the fairy path wound through a thicket of balsam trees. He paused, then looked back and barked, as if to make sure we were following.

"Come on, Clara. You'll be warmer if we walk. I promise it's not far. You'll see."

I took her hand, and we stumbled up the hill, our shoes squishing with water. When we reached the top, I pointed to our house, just a short distance away. Smoke billowed from the chimney. "There's a fire going in the stove. We'll be warm and cozy soon. Mom will make us hot tea, and you'll get into clean, dry clothes." I talked almost constantly, to encourage Clara but also to keep myself from thinking about the cold, wet clothes that clung to me and the smarting scratches on my own hands and legs.

When we were halfway down the other slope, Blizzard ran off to the house, barking. The door opened and Mom peered out.

"Mom!" I yelled. "It's me and Clara!" I walked faster, pulling Clara along.

Mom ran toward us. "What happened? Where . . . ? Did you walk all the way from the Harbor?" She reached us, then stopped, her mouth gaping. "You're both soaking. What on earth happened? Why is Clara here?" She bent down and took Clara's hands in hers.

"My child, you are freezing." She took off her sweater and wrapped it around Clara. "Come, get in the house both of you and I'll warm up some dry clothes. Oh my! I can't imagine—"

"Oh, Mom. So much happened in Gull Harbor. I couldn't wait for Dad to come for me tomorrow." I stammered on and on, trying to tell Mom everything at once. "Mike Hawley fell off the wharf under a ship. . . . He's hurt bad, and his father blames me. Clara was in the barn. . . . I couldn't leave her there. And then we fell into the brook. . . . Blizzard saved Clara."

"It's all right, Jessie," Mom said gently. "You can tell me all about it, but now you must change your clothes and have some hot tea." We had reached the house, and Mom called Blizzard. "Come in, Blizzard. You need to get dry and warm too." She patted my dog as he trotted into the house, his tail wagging.

I laughed a little, and the tears that were waiting slipped down my cheeks. "See, Clara? I told you Mom would take good care of us and make everything better."

CHAPTER 17

The Water-Horse

When Mom pulled off Clara's dirty, wet clothing, she gasped. "What are these?" she asked, pointing to the red welts on Clara's legs.

"I got scratched on the rocks," Clara answered.

"No, I don't mean the fresh ones. I'm talking about these older bruises."

"Pa whipped me with his belt," Clara said. "I wasn't doing the dishes like I was told."

Mom grabbed Clara and hugged her, but her eyes were on me. She nodded slightly, and I knew she understood why I had had to bring Clara back to our house.

Mom took the two of us into the back kitchen where we kept our big tin bathtub. She filled it with balmy water from the stove and gave Clara a soothing bath. Then, while Mom toweled Clara down and dressed her in one of my old sweatshirts, I climbed into the warm sudsy water. I unbraided my long hair and rinsed the sticky sugar out of it, and then sank deep into the water. My cuts and bruises stung at first, but before long the pain eased away.

Soon we were warm, dry, and bundled up before the fire. Blizzard stretched out on his blanket, a paw in every direction. "Thank you for saving Clara, our sweet, wonderful dog," Mom said to him as she rubbed him down with a towel.

I told her everything over the tea and muffins and bakeapple jam that she saved for special occasions. Gran entered the kitchen in her regal way. "That dog smells when he's wet. Put him out," she commanded.

"No," Mom said. "He saved Clara's life."

"And Mike Hawley's, too," I reminded her.

Mr. Blair came into the room and listened to our stories, including Clara's sad tale of the beatings and cruelty by the McCrumbs. Then I gave all the details about Mike Hawley and how he pestered me and fell into the water.

Gran, as usual, didn't say much, and I couldn't tell what she was thinking by her lack of expression. As Mom had said many times, "Gran always keeps her feelings tucked in her heart." I sometimes wondered if she had any heart at all.

Mr. Blair, however, was furious to hear of Clara's

abuse. He was worried, too, about Mike's fall. "How bad is he, Jessie; do you know?"

"His arm is badly hurt. Oh, I wish I had never stayed over in Gull Harbor. Maybe Mike would be all right if I hadn't."

"Jessie, Mike always gets in trouble. He's that kind of kid," Mom said.

"Everyone knows that boy is a bullamarue," Gran added.

"And if Jessie hadn't stayed in the harbor, Clara wouldn't be here. And she needed to get out of there," Mom said to Mr. Blair.

"Jack Hawley says Dad will have to pay for Mike's injuries," I told her.

"Why should he?" Gran demanded.

"Dad will take care of everything, Jessie; don't you worry," Mom said gently. "He'll be back soon. He's out in the boat with Donald Anderson."

I was real happy that Mr. Blair, Uncle Don, and Ned hadn't left for St. John's yet. Now I'd have a chance to see Ned again before he went home. Mom told me that Erik had taken Ned fishing in the punt.

Mr. Blair was fascinated by Clara's fear of the each-uisge, which he pronounced *ach ishkeh*. "The word is Gaelic for a creature from Celtic folklore—the most dangerous of any water-dwelling creatures," he explained. "It looks like a beautiful horse, but it can change into many forms. Usually it tries to drown anyone who approaches or tries to ride it. I'm surprised that Clara knows about it."

"Henrietta McCrumb scared her with all sorts of stories," I answered. "Gran told me the stories of the water-horse, but they never scared me. I knew they were all pishogue!"

Mr. Blair was quiet for a moment, then said, "Hmm, I suppose it's just a superstition. Yet look what happened after you both saw the creature."

I was shocked to hear Mr. Blair suggest the pony was a water creature. "It was a Newfoundland pony," I insisted. "Clara said one was missing from the corral that Melloy built."

"He built a corral?" Gran spoke up suddenly. "Why?"

"I don't know. But he seems to be gathering some of the ponies that were abandoned."

Gran sniffed. "Humph. I'm sure he's got something up his sleeve. Next thing he'll be over here after Clara. What will you do then?" She directed her question to Mom.

"We'll cross that bridge when we come to it," Mom said.

"Don't send me back, please," Clara begged tearfully. "Let me stay with you and Jessie. If I go back now . . . they'll . . ." She began to sob.

"Hush, my child. Everything will be all right." Mom sat on the big rocking chair, gathered Clara into her arms and began to rock, singing the old Scottish lullaby she had sung to me many times. I didn't understand the ancient Gaelic words, but the music was comforting, and as I watched, Clara's eyes closed, and I could tell she had fallen asleep.

Gaelic words. I thought of the old Celtic superstition—the each-uisge. Yet there had been the form of a horse in the mist and shadows by the brook. I had seen it too. It vanished as soon as we'd sighted it. Then Clara fell into the water and almost drowned.

I felt creepy gooseflesh around my neck and down my arms. *It's pishogue!* I told myself. That wasn't an evil fairy pony. It was real. I'll find him and bring him back here and show him to Clara. Then she'll know he isn't haunted and things will be all right. I had it all figured out, and then . . . I don't even remember climbing onto the couch, but soon I was fast asleep.

CHAPTER 18

Trouble Ahead

It was still Sunday, but night already, when I awoke. I could hear men's voices mixing into my dream—Dad's and Uncle Don's. Sometimes Erik and Ned laughed softly. I realized I had been asleep for a long time. How long I didn't know, but it was after supper, because I could hear Mom washing dishes, and the smell of turnip and onions drifted from the kitchen. Clara had cuddled up with me on my couch, and her face and golden hair were pale against the white pillow. *Poor little girl*, I thought, as I untangled myself from the blanket, trying not to awaken her.

Everyone was eating sponge cake smothered in jelly and tinned cream when I walked in and stood next to Dad's place.

"Oh, Jessie, my poor little child. What a time you've had down in Gull Harbor." Dad got up to hug me, and suddenly I wanted to climb into his lap as I had when I was little. But I knew I would cry. Instead I tried to be calm and brave as I pulled up a chair next to him.

"Dad, it was awful. I just had to come home."

"Mom told us everything," he replied.

"Did you hear about Mike Hawley's terrible accident? And how his dad blamed me?"

Dad nodded.

"Did Mom tell you how Clara was beaten and locked up in the barn? I had to get her away from the McCrumbs, Dad. I couldn't wait for you to come for me on Monday. I decided to walk home on the fairy path." My voice shook tearfully.

Dad put his arm around me. "Jessie, Mike Hawley's accident was never your fault. And don't worry about Clara. We'll keep her here."

Uncle Don spoke up. "In the meantime I'll find out at my government office in St. John's if there are any records that give custody of Clara to the McCrumbs I'll find a legal way to take her away from them."

"I've heard her last name is Cadigan, but I don't think anyone, even Clara, is really sure," I said, wiping away a tear that slipped down my cheek.

"Don't cry anymore, my child," Dad said. "Clara's parents may have died, but the rest of the family didn't just disappear off the face of the earth."

I nodded and sniffed.

"Now, hush, Jessie," Gran said. "You're almost fourteen. Don't act like a baby."

"Jessie did *not* act like a baby. She did a very brave thing by saving Clara," Dad said with a stern look at Gran. "Now she's home and safe and very hungry, right?" Dad patted my hand. "Gran saved your supper in the oven."

I avoided Gran's eyes when she took a plate of food from the oven and placed it in front of me. I picked up my fork and dug it into the mashed turnip and beef. I hadn't realized how hungry I was until I took the first bite. Blizzard whined and pawed at my leg. "Blizzard's hungry too. Did Mom tell you how he saved Clara?"

"That dog is right clever," Mr. Blair said, patting Blizzard's head. "We owe him our lives."

Mom smiled. "And he's been treated royally, let me tell. He's already had his own big plate of supper."

"I was afraid Melloy McCrumb would chase us through the woods," I said. "But I knew Blizzard would protect us."

"I'm sure no one would dare lay a hand on either of you with Blizzard there," said Ned.

"Do you think anyone believes I pushed Mike off the wharf?" I asked.

"Mike's always been a bullamarue," Erik stated, trying to be comforting. "What happened serves him right."

"Hush!" Gran scolded. "That's a horrible thing to say. Even Mike Hawley doesn't deserve to have such a terrible accident."

"Yes, Erik, that kid has always been a troublemaker," Dad agreed, ignoring Gran. "This time he went too far, and hopefully learned a lesson, sad as it may be." Dad turned to me. "You and Clara will be safe here at the Cliffs."

"But what about tomorrow? Aren't you taking the Andersons to White Falls to get the train? Are you well enough to travel, Mr. Blair?" Mom asked.

"I'm fine, thanks to all the good care I've had here." Mr. Blair smiled at Gran.

"Just the same, you'll be seeing a doctor soon as we get home," Uncle Don told him.

"Then we'll be all alone here tomorrow," I said anxiously.

"Erik will be here, maid," Dad said, "and your mom and Gran. Besides, I don't think Melloy McCrumb would dare show up here and face us. He knows that we're aware of what he's done to Clara and that she has the bruises to show for it."

"What about Jack Hawley? He came over to the Doyles' house looking for me."

"He's way off at Bird Cliff Hospital with his son. But I'll stop on the way back and get a feel of what's happening in Gull Harbor," Dad replied. "It should be interesting."

Gran spoke up. "Don't go and get into a fight down there."

Dad laughed out loud. "Since when have I ever been in a fight? Name one time."

"Never since I've known you." Mom laughed too. "Your words have more power than fists! Why, you can talk a school of cod into a net."

Gran frowned. "There's trouble ahead; I can feel it in my bones." The men at the table chuckled, and I could see Gran getting angry. "For one thing, that child sleepin' in there doesn't belong to us."

"Don't fear, Mrs. Wheller," Uncle Don said gently. "I'll see to it that your family will not get into trouble for saving Clara."

Still, I knew Gran was right. There was trouble ahead. We'd be hearing from Melloy McCrumb and Jack Hawley very soon.

CHAPTER 19

Plans for the Ponies

Clara woke up just a little later. She came out to the kitchen drowsily and climbed into Mom's lap. "Jessie, get Clara some dinner from the oven. I'm sure she's half starved—aren't you, my child?" She kissed Clara on the forehead.

I fixed Clara a bowl of potatoes, turnips, and beef, covered it all with gravy, then placed it on the table. She looked up at me gratefully, and after settling into a chair she began to eat. Gran poured a glass of milk and placed it in front of Clara. "Thank you," Clara said softly.

Gran paused and gazed at Clara for a long moment and then, without speaking, she turned away.

Clara's sweetness would melt even an iceberg, I thought. *But Gran is so cold she could scare the scales off a fish. Still,* I recalled, *when I was sick with the chin cough and burning up with fever, she bathed me down and rubbed my back.* Yet she never said much or sang to me, like Mom. *Mayhap Gran's a crimbil herself.*

Crimbils were never happy in the mortal world, I'd been told.

As we all sat by the stove, Mr. Blair spoke about the old days in Last Chance. "The fish were so thick there wasn't room for them all in the sea." He laughed. "You could walk across the bay on their backs."

"You're sounding like an October Gailer," Uncle Don kidded. "Next thing you'll be bragging about your survival in that rogue storm . . ."

"And how the waves were fifty feet high," Ned added.

Erik guffawed. "Listen. If you're goin' to be an October Gailer, you might as well make it a really good story. Ninety-foot waves sound about right. And the winds . . . I'd say a hundred fifty miles per hour."

"What's an October Gailer?" I asked.

"A braggart," Mom answered. "Someone who exaggerates the truth."

"It comes from the old days, when one of the last fishing boats would come home from the Labrador in October with blown-up tales of wild storms," Mr. Blair said.

"Most fishin' crews were back in home port by then, so there was no one to deny the stories," Dad added, then turned back to Mr. Blair. "But the storm that took you down was really bad, and that ain't a tale!"

"That's right," Erik said. "You'll have a whale of a story to tell about your shipwreck when you get back to St. John's."

"The trouble is, no one will believe us!" Mr. Blair exclaimed. "They'll think we're all . . ."

"October Gailers!" the men said in unison, and then burst out laughing.

Mom turned to Clara. "Do you have any stories to tell, Clara? You didn't always live with the McCrumbs, did you?"

Clara looked down at her hands and shook her head. "I only remember bits and pieces from when I was very little."

"Do you recall any relatives? Your real parents? Aunts and uncles?" Mr. Anderson asked. Clara shook her head. "Ma McCrumb says all my folks died from the TB."

"Tuberculosis." Dad nodded. "Lots of that out on the Labrador. Perhaps she's from there."

"Then you've lived with the McCrumbs most of your life?" Mom asked.

Clara nodded and looked up at Mom with anxious eyes. "I don't want to go back. Please don't send me back!"

"We'll do our best to keep you here with us," Mom promised.

"Unless we can find your real family," Mr. Anderson said. "Would you like that?"

"I don't know my real family. Besides, I might not like them as well as you."

"That's enough questions," Gran said. "Leave the child alone."

"You're right, Mrs. Wheller," Mr. Anderson agreed. He turned to me. "Are you going to look for that mystery horse tomorrow?"

"I might. It was a very pretty Newfoundland pony; wasn't it, Clara?" Clara sank lower in her chair and didn't answer. "I only got a glimpse," I continued, "but it looked something like Raven. Dark brown with a black mane. I think it escaped from Melloy McCrumb's new fenced-in pen he's built."

"He's built a pen for the horses?" Dad asked. "When did this happen?"

"Just recently. The wood he used was newly cut," I told him.

Dad frowned. "What does he plan to do with the horses?"

"Clara says he's tellin' folks that he and Jack are rescuing 'em off the islands."

Clara suddenly cut in. "I know 'sactly what he said. He said he's going to fatten them up and send them to Quebec."

"What? Fatten them up?" Dad jumped up and slammed his fist on the table. "I know what he's got in mind. He's . . ."

"Walt!" Mom interrupted, sending Dad a warning look. She put her finger to her lips. "Whist! The children."

Dad stopped speaking. Then he sat down again. At first Mr. Anderson and Mr. Blair appeared to be puzzled. Then they nodded, and I could see that they understood what I didn't.

"What's goin' on?" I demanded. "Tell me." I looked from one person to the other, but everyone, including Erik and Ned, avoided my stare.

"Nothin' for you to think about, dear," Mom finally said.

Nothing, indeed! When would they stop treating me like a child? I knew right well that something bad was going to happen to the horses in Quebec. But what?

CHAPTER 20

Saying Good-bye

Everyone was up early the next morning. Clara, who shared my couch, whispered close to my ear, "Wake up, Jessie." There was a bright, happy smile on her face. She looked cute in an old shirt of mine that came to her knees. "Let's get up, Jessie."

In the kitchen Mom had tea brewing. Erik brought in fresh eggs from our henhouse and scrambled them in a big bowl. Gran was busy toasting bread on the stove. She sprinkled the first piece with cinnamon and sugar and handed it to Clara.

"This is a big day." Uncle Don grinned as he came into the kitchen dressed in his own clothes that Mom had washed and ironed. "We'll be going home at last—after a very pleasant rescue by the Wheller family."

"Well, we're right happy that everything turned out well—in spite of a frightening shipwreck," Mom said.

Erik and Ned sat at the table. "I'll miss you, Ned," Erik said. "There won't be any fun without you around."

I wanted to tell Ned I'd miss him too, but I blushed even thinking about saying it. Instead I said, "I hope you'll come back in the summer and we'll all go berrying."

"And we can fish together," Erik added.

"I'm lookin' forward to it," Ned said, "as long as your folks wouldn't mind."

"Ned, we think of you as another son," Dad said. "You'll be welcome here at the Cliffs anytime—and so will your father and grandfather. You're all part of our family."

I put my arm around Clara's shoulder. "And so are you, Clara. From now on you are my little sister."

Clara smiled, and this time her little nose wrinkled up. I had never noticed that before, probably 'cause she'd never had anything to be up in cheers about. I glanced quickly at Gran and actually caught her smiling at Clara.

Before we sat down to scrambled eggs, homemade sausage, tea, and toast, Dad asked the blessing. I held Clara's hand as he prayed. "Thank you, Lord, our shepherd, for this family and for our friends who came to us in the storm. Thank you for delivering them, and please watch over them as they travel today. Thank you for bringing little Clara to us for safety, and we pray that she will be able to stay with us under your guiding care."

"Amen," we all agreed.

"Now," Dad said as he dug into the eggs, "the plan today is for us to get off to White Falls as quickly as we can. Erik, I want you to bide here. I need a man to be with the family while I'm gone. Howsomever, I could use help watchin' for rocks on the way back, as the tide may be going out by then, so I'm thinking Mom should come along with us. She knows the tickle right well. How does that sound?"

"I suppose it will be all right," Mom said hesitantly, "as long as the girls will be safe." She looked worried.

I dreaded the thought of the McCrumbs or the Hawleys showing up. "Maybe we should all go with you."

Dad shook his head. "I'm stoppin' at Gull Harbor for gas and to see what's goin' on. You don't want to go back there, do you?

"No, Dad," I said quickly. "Clara and I will bide here with Erik and Gran. We'll be all right."

Uncle Don and Mr. Blair looked at each other, and worried frowns creased their foreheads. "We're sorry to take your dad off like this," Uncle Don said to me.

"We'll be just fine," I replied. "We're alone most of the summer, when Dad goes off to the Labrador to fish." I sounded brave, but I was afeared of Melloy McCrumb and Jack Hawley coming after Clara and me.

Later I felt right sad to see the Anderson family go. Before they left, Ned and Erik exchanged addresses.

"I hope you'll both write to me," Ned said. "I'll miss this place . . . and all the excitement around here."

"Don't forget, you're comin' back this summer for a visit," I said.

"Come as soon as school's out," Erik said. "But come before Dad and I head off to the Labrador."

"I will," Ned promised. "Soon as school lets out for the summer."

Dad had written down Uncle Don's home and office address and telephone numbers. How I wished we had telephones.

After they were gone, I went upstairs and spruced up my room and claimed my own bed! Still, I'd miss Mr. Blair, too, and his stories of Celtic legends. I hoped he'd come back someday and tell us more about the fairies and the water-horses . . . the each-uisge. It was strange that Clara knew so much about them too. The McCrumbs sure scared her with those fairy tales.

Clara and I helped Gran clean up the kitchen, and then we played hide-the-slipper with my shoe. Clara laughed and giggled when it was her turn to hide it and I couldn't find it. I wondered if she had ever played a game in all her born days.

I took her out to meet Raven in the barn. "I may let Raven run free today," I told her. "The weather's nice and airsome."

"You'll be happy to be free, won't you, Raven?" Clara said, stroking Raven's neck. "You and I have both been locked up in the barn, and now we can run and play."

I opened the stall door and led Raven outside. "It's all right, little girl," I said, unhooking her bridle. "Off you go."

Raven snorted and stepped around cautiously. Then she made a little leap and ran off into the pasture. Clara and I watched and laughed as she pranced, rolled over in the dirt, and galloped over the meadow.

"Will she run away?" Clara asked me.

"She won't go far. She knows this is her home. I'll pen her up later. She wants to roam around for now."

I heard the sound of a motor on the westerly wind.

Someone was coming. I froze, then grabbed Clara's hand and ran into the house. "Gran! Where's Erik?"

"I don't know. Wasn't he with you?"

"No, and I hear a boat comin' into the barrasway. It might be the McCrumbs!"

Clara let out a little scream and burst into tears. "They've come for me!"

"Hush, child," Gran said calmly. "We don't know it's them."

"Hide, Clara!" I yelled. "Hide!"

"Where?" Clara whimpered.

"Stop!" Gran put her hand up. "Let's not get all afeared when—"

"Gran, she has to—"

"Jessie, stop talkin' and run to the top of the barrasway. See who's coming. Then we'll know what to do."

"But Clara—"

"Go!" Gran said. "I'll take care of Clara."

CHAPTER 21

A Warning

I ran out toward our little harbor. A small boat was pulling up to the wharf. It was the Doyles! *What are they doing here?* I wondered. I felt relieved, but still we had to hide Clara. I flew back to the house. "It's the Doyles!"

"Well, see? Nothin' to be ascared about," Gran said.

"But they mustn't know Clara's here," I insisted. "No one should know. Then no one can tell."

"Very well," Gran said, surprising me. "Clara, go up into a bedroom and shut the door. Don't come out until we tell you. And not a yap out of you!"

Clara nodded and raced up the stairway. I could hear her footsteps and then a door shutting just as Auntie Liz and Uncle Pete Doyle came up the walkway.

I met them at the door. "Hi! What a nice surprise," I said. "I hope you're not upset because I left so quick yesterday. You did get my note, didn't you?"

"Yes, Jessie, we did. Thank you. We would have

worried otherwise." Auntie Liz turned to my grand-mother. "Hello, Mrs. Wheller."

Gran simply nodded as she stood as straight as a rampike, her hands folded.

"Please come in." I gestured to the settle and chairs. "Don't make strange. Will you have some tea?"

"Thanks, Jessie." Auntie Liz looked around and then sat at the table. "Where are your folks?"

Uncle Pete took the rocker. "Yes. We hoped they'd be here."

"They've taken the Andersons to White Falls, where they'll take a train back to St. John's," I explained. "Dad and Mom won't be back until late."

Gran poured tea into mugs and placed them on the table. "Is there anything we can help you with?" she asked. "We don't see you often out these parts."

"That's true, Mrs. Wheller." Auntie Liz looked uncomfortable as she helped herself to the tea. "Did you know that little Clara Cadigan disappeared yes-terday?"

"Oh, did she?" Gran said.

Uncle Pete reached for his tea, then settled back into the rocker. "No one knows where she is or if she's all right."

As I glanced back and forth from the Doyles to Gran, I noticed the basket of laundry on a chair. Neatly folded on the top was a little sweater that had been mine and was obviously too small for me now. I gasped and then pretended to cough. Gran must have understood, because she glanced quickly at the laundry, then turned away.

"Didn't she go to church with the McCrumbs yesterday?" I asked, trying my best to look innocent.

"No, they said they left Clara home in bed because she wasn't feeling well," Auntie Liz replied. "When they got back to the house, Clara was gone. Henrietta is heartbroken with worry."

Home in bed? Mrs. McCrumb heartbroken? I wanted to yell out the truth. I glanced over at Gran, who sat quietly sipping tea. But her eyes caught mine, and I could see she was fuming too.

"If Clara ran away, I wouldn't blame her," I said, unable to control myself completely. "I've seen Henrietta McCrumb shove her around. And my friends told me Clara goes to school without lunch lots of times!"

"That's probably true," Auntie Liz admitted. "But the reason we came, Jessie . . . oh, dear, how can I put it." She took a deep breath. "Jessie, the McCrumbs are saying you kidnapped Clara. They're coming over here this afternoon. Everyone in town was searching Gull Harbor until dark last night. Now they're combing the woods to see if they can find her. The folks from the Harbor could show up here at any time."

Uncle Pete nodded. "We wanted to warn you—in case you know where she is."

"I don't know where she is," I said quickly. It wasn't really a lie. I didn't know in which bedroom she was hiding.

To my astonishment, Gran went over to the laundry basket, picked up the little sweater, opened it up, shook it a little, and then folded it up slowly and carefully. "I'm sure Clara is being well taken care of—wherever she is. And it would be such a shame to send her back to be beaten and mistreated, wouldn't it?"

The Doyles looked at each other and settled back in their chairs. "As long as Clara is safe, I'm certain no one in town would want her to go back to the McCrumbs," Auntie Liz said.

"That's true," Uncle Pete agreed. "The child should never have gone to the McCrumbs in the first place, so why should she go back to them if someone is taking good care of her?"

"And why would *anyone* tell those McCrumbs where she was?" Gran added. "If anyone knew, that is."

"No one needs to know where Clara is, as long as everyone is assured she is safe," Auntie Liz replied. "Of course . . . we don't know where she is . . ."

"And wherever she is, you can be certain she's as safe as a little bird in a nest," Gran said.

I was upset and relieved at the same time. Although the Doyles wouldn't reveal Clara's whereabouts, they'd assure the townspeople that she was safe.

"One more thing, though. The McCrumbs are sure you took her, Jessie. So be careful what you say or do—especially since your folks are away," Auntie Liz warned.

"Melloy and Henrietta are upset. Very upset," Uncle Pete added. "You see, the McCrumbs get a check every month from some relative of Clara's who lives in Toronto. So . . ."

Auntie Liz cut in. "Every month without fail they spend money on themselves . . . as if it's as plentiful as beach rocks."

"The McCrumbs don't care one bit about Clara, but I'm sure they do care about that money," Gran stated.

"Clara must have a family, if someone is sending money," I said. "Who are they?"

"No one knows—except the McCrumbs," Uncle Pete said.

"They sure don't spend it on Clara!" I told them about the coat and hat I'd given Clara and how I saw another girl wearing them.

"Figures. They probably sold them." Uncle Pete stood up.

"How is Mike Hawley?" I had to know before they left.

"We haven't seen the Hawleys lately," Uncle Pete answered. "They've been at the hospital with Mike. I hear he's holding his own."

Auntie Liz got up and headed for the door. "I'm certainly glad that Clara's out of harm's way and hidden where they won't find her."

"In the meantime, until we tell neighbors she's safe, they'll be out here soon searching the woods and shoreline," Uncle Pete put in.

"No need to worry about the Harbor folks; we'll take care of that. But be on the watch, Mrs. Wheller, and you too, Jessie," Auntie Liz advised as she opened the door. "The McCrumbs will be here soon, and they're on the rampage. Don't tell them we came to tip you off."

"We won't," I promised. "Thanks for warnin' us."

"Won't they see your boat on the way back?" Gran asked.

"We'll be back before they leave Gull Harbor," Uncle Pete said. "We came by way of the tickle during low tide. They won't come in their big boat until the tide turns. They're afraid of the sunkers. But the people who are searchin' the woods may arrive anytime." The Doyles waved good-bye and headed back down the path to our harbor.

"You as much as told the Doyles that Clara's here," I accused Gran. "And now the McCrumbs are comin' out here. What'll we do? And where is Erik when we need him?"

"I don't know, my child," Gran answered. "But whether Erik is here or not, I won't let anyone take Clara. You can be sure of that!"

CHAPTER 22

Searchers

My grandmother was standing at the door, her arms crossed. Then she turned suddenly and slammed the door. "The McCrumbs will be showing up here pretty soon."

"What shall we do?"

"Right now we've got to hide Clara—and everything that belongs to her," she said, picking up the little sweater. "They'd spot things like this straightaway."

"What will we tell them?"

"Leave that to me." Gran said. "Clara!" she called. "Come on down now and clean up everything that's yours." She grabbed Clara's coloring book and crayons from a nearby table. "We missed these," she said as she stuffed them into a sack. "Jessie, you go find Erik." Gran was suddenly a general in command of an army.

Just as I opened the door, Erik appeared from the fairy path—with Raven in tow. "Here comes Erik, Gran." I called. "He must have been out searching for Raven. I let her out to pasture this morning."

Gran came out and looked around. "But isn't that Raven over there by the barn?" she asked, pointing to our horse grazing in the meadow.

As he came closer, Erik waved and shouted, "This is your demon horse! He's as tame as a kitten! I think he's Raven's twin brother! I'm putting him in the barn."

"Is there enough hay for another horse?" Gran called out.

"Enough for a herd!" Erik answered.

By now Clara had joined us. "He found the each-uisge?" she whispered. "Don't let it come near me!"

"It's just another horse," I said. "See how sweet he is?" But Clara pulled back from the door fearfully.

"That each-uisge talk is a lot of pishogue!" Gran said angrily. When Clara's eyes filled with tears, she spoke in a softer tone. "Listen, my child, we have no time for tears. We have to get you away from here before the McCrumbs arrive." She lifted Clara's face up. "Now, are you going to sit here and cry over that gentle beast out there? Or are you goin' to do as I say?"

Clara nodded over and over. "I'll do as you say."

"Erik!" Gran yelled. "Get Raven saddled up the

once. I'm sending you and Clara out to Lonesome Isle before the tide turns. It's best for her to be away from here when they come. Now hurry!"

I was stunned! *Lonesome Isle?* Even Erik stopped in his path and looked comical struck.

We never went out to that sad, haunted place. I wanted to argue, but I couldn't for fear of scaring Clara.

Clara grabbed my hand. "Please come with us, Jessie. I want you to come."

"Jessie can't ride Raven out in the tickle, especially with the tide turning. Raven will need a strong hand, and only Erik can do that." Gran's lips were in a straight line, and I knew she was determined.

I had to admit to myself that Gran's plan was shocking perfect. No one would suspect any one of us would go out to Lonesome Isle. After all, that was where most of our family perished—and where the ghosts still cried out. People of Gull Harbor steered clear of that place, which had dangerous rocks on the seaside and the rocky tickle on our side. It would be a great place to hide.

"I'll take Clara," I said.

"No! It's too dangerous. You two little maids on a

horse? Crossing at tide change?" Gran had her hands on her hips. "Absolutely not!"

"Gran, when are you going to realize I am not little anymore? I'm almost fourteen. And I'm a good rider—" She turned away, and I grabbed her arm.

"Stop that!" Gran snapped, spinning around.

Clara started to cry, and suddenly I was angry. "Gran, you're frightening Clara. I hate to say it, but you sound very much like Henrietta McCrumb when you yell at me." I almost bit my tongue when I realized those words had come out of my mouth. "Oh, I'm sorry, Gran. Please forgive me." I put my arms around Gran, but I could feel her stiffen, so I stepped back. "Dad said you must have Erik here when the McCrumbs come. So let's do what Dad says."

There was a long pause, and then she threw her hands up. "Then get going and hurry up about it. The tide's changing all the while you're standing here quarrelling with me."

Erik had led the other horse to the barn, and I could see Raven watching from the pasture. I wondered if he would be able to saddle her up now that she'd had her spring taste of freedom.

Meanwhile Gran threw together apples, a thermos of hot tea, and some dry clothes. "Bundle up!" she ordered Clara as she stuffed everything into one of Dad's nunny bags. "You too, Jessie."

"Where are we goin'?" Clara asked as I helped her into warm clothes.

"Just out to that pretty island," I said. "No one will ever think we were out there."

"Why not? Won't they look for us there?" Clara asked.

"Not likely. The island is deserted." I wasn't about to scare Clara with the tales of ghosts and hollies.

I hastily pulled on my snowsuit jacket and hat, and then we all headed out to the barn, where Erik was waiting. Raven stood at the door, saddled. She was frisky as a pup and hopping around impatiently. Blizzard was standing by, watching, his tail wagging.

"No, you can't go, Blizzard," Gran said.

"You stay here and guard Gran and Erik." I patted his head.

"What are you sayin'?" Erik asked. "Ain't I goin' over to the island?"

"No, you need to stay here with Gran," I told him. "Those were Dad's orders. You heard him yourself."

Erik looked concerned. "But what about you, Jessie—on that island by yourselves. You know the stories."

"Pishogue!" I gave him a warning look and a nod toward Clara.

"I mean . . . I sure hopes Raven will . . . er . . . be obedient," Erik added quickly.

"She'll be fine with me riding," I said. "Clara's heard how much Raven loves me."

Suddenly, we heard dogs barking from the woods. "Hurry up," Gran said. "The search party will be here any moment now."

I climbed into the saddle, and Erik lifted Clara behind me. "What's all this fuss about, anyway?" he asked Gran.

"There's a search party on their way through the woods for Clara, and the McCrumbs are comin' by boat," Gran answered. "We've got to get the girls out of here."

"Why don't we just stand up to them all and tell them the truth?" Erik said. "That Clara's been beaten and left in the barn—"

"Henrietta is grief-stricken," Gran said mockingly. "She's probably already talked the whole town into believing her. And with all the gossip about Mike Hawley . . ." Gran placed the nunny bag tightly between Clara and me and then waved us toward the barrasway. "Get going, Jessie!"

The barking of dogs sounded closer. I clicked my heel lightly on Raven's flank, and she began to walk toward the water. "We're crossing from the beach on the point," I told Gran and Erik. "It's closer to the island and away from the barrasway, where the McCrumbs will land."

"Hurry! Your dad will come get you when it's safe to come home!" Gran called after us. "Be careful, my girls."

I clicked my heel again and could feel Clara's arms tighten around my waist. "Let's go, Raven!"

Raven's walk turned into a trot and then a gallop as we raced toward the beach and Lonesome Isle.

CHAPTER 23

Escape to Lonesome Isle

As swift as a raven, my pony flew down the rough pathway, her hooves clicking on the stones and rocks. "Hang on, Clara!" I could feel her face against my back, and I wondered if she was frightened. So far she'd been brave and trusting. Did she trust me enough to cross the water with me, after she fell into the rushing brook?

We had reached the sandy point, and Raven slowed to a walk, as if wondering what she should do next. I clicked my heels and urged her toward the water. "It's all right, Raven." I stroked her neck. "You can do it, my love," I whispered. "We need you, girl, to save Clara. Only you can help us, Raven." My horse cocked an ear, and somehow I knew she understood.

The surface of the water was still, but there was a slight churning around the tops of the sunkers. The tide was about to change.

"Giddap, Raven," I said. "Go on!" I tapped my heels on her sides again, and she started into the water, but, uncertain of her footing, she stopped and tried to turn back. "Go! Good girl!" I reached forward, patted her neck once more. "Giddap!" I ordered again.

This time Raven headed out into the water, walking slowly and cautiously over the slippery rocks. I could feel her slide now and then as she lost her foothold. But gradually she made her way out into the deeper water. Suddenly, I felt her body surge smoothly as she began to swim.

Our legs were now submerged in the icy water. "Are you all right, Clara?" I asked. She hadn't said a word since we began our ride.

"I'm just holdin' on, Jessie. I don't want to see where we are."

After a few minutes I felt the rhythmic motion of Raven's swim change back to a struggling walk as she approached the shore of Lonesome Isle. Soon my wonderful horse had us safely on the stony beach. "Good girl, Raven!" I crooned as I dismounted and helped Clara onto the ground. "You were so brave, Clara. I'm right proud of you."

"I kept my eyes closed," she said with a grin. "I got really ascared when I felt the water coming up around me."

I handed the nunny bag to Clara and took hold of Raven's bridle. "Come on, you right clever girl," I said. "We need to hide you somewhere so's no one can see you from the tickle."

Raven flicked her head and shook, spraying drops of salt water around us. Our soaking pants clung to our legs, and our shoes squished as we made our way up over the smooth stones to higher ground.

Above the beach Gran's old gray house, where my dad was born, was now sadly falling apart. Beyond was an overgrown meadow, where the horse, cows, and sheep had grazed. The barn still stood at the foot of a hill that rose abruptly out of the low-lying trees. It felt dreamlike and strange—as if by coming we'd gone back in time.

"I'm so cold and wet, Jessie." Clara's teeth chattered as she spoke.

"Aye. Let's go to the barn and put on the dry clothes Gran sent along."

As we headed through the deep grass to the barn, I was amazed at the number of overgrown berry bushes. *In the summertime this would be a wonderful place to pick berries*, I thought. Then I remembered the hollies, and felt gooseflesh crawl up my arms and neck.

"Have you been here before, Jessie?" Clara asked through her bivvering lips.

"Dad's been out here a few times and brought back berries." I didn't tell her about the sad memories here on the island. "Maybe we'll come again when the berries are ripe."

The large barn seemed strong, despite the many years it had weathered pounding storms and wind. The faint smell of musty wood and manure still drifted through the stalls. I'd heard that Gran had a few cows and a couple of sheep and horses, but I never realized how many she must have had here. There were ten or fifteen stalls in the old place.

While Clara pulled out dry clothes and changed, I tied Raven to a post with the reins and rubbed her down with a rag I found. "We don't want you to catch cold, Raven," I crooned. "Thank you for bringin' us here safely." Raven snorted softly, then rubbed her head on my arm.

"She loves you." Clara smiled as she pulled a dry sweater over her head. "I love you too, Jessie. You are my best friend." But when her head popped out through the top of the sweater, her smile was gone. "Do you think Mom and Pa will come out here to get me?"

"No, they'd never think of us bein' out here, and Gran and Erik won't let on where we are." I didn't dare tell Clara about the ghosts. Evidently she had never heard the stories about this island.

I changed, stretched out our wet clothing along the wall of one of the stalls, and then pulled out the hot tea and apples. We sat on old half-keg barrels and sipped on the tea right out of the thermos, since we had no cups. After eating, Clara seemed up in cheers and even giggled as she fed Raven our apple cores.

I stood up and stretched. "Now that we're warm, let's find the gull gaze. It's a lookout that Dad talks about. That's where his pa used to hide out to shoot birds. It's hidden among the trees so the birds wouldn't be scared away."

"Then it will be a good place for us to hide too," Clara said.

I wanted to let Raven loose to graze, but I was fearful she might be spotted by anyone on the shore. So I closed her into a large stall. "Sorry, Raven," I told her.

Clara and I went into the tuckamore and began our climb up the small but steep hill behind the barn.

"Look at this," I said to Clara. "Someone has done target shooting out here." I bent over and picked up old bullet shells. Nailed up on a tree was a faded target with a bull's-eye that had been practically wiped out by bullets. "Someone must be a right good shot to have hit this target so well," I added.

The balsam trees were so thick it was hard to move, but we managed to push our way through until we found the narrow path that led to the top of the hill.

It was afternoon now, and the sun was balmy. The refreshing smell of fir trees mixed with the salty breeze. We climbed higher, pausing now and then to rest, or to find the best way to climb over the smooth, bald rock face of the knoll. Stony Tickle spread out below us, and the cliffs to the east of our house reached up high above the sea.

Soon we reached the gull gaze. It was just as my dad had described it. What a pretty place! The winding dark water of the tickle was before us. On the other side the blue ocean stretched out to the horizon. We were well hidden as we sat behind small trees that had grown out of the crevices of soil in the rock.

"Look! There's a boat pulled up to our wharf," I whispered to Clara, pointing to our dock. "And it's not my dad and mom."

Clara grabbed my arm and ducked down. "No,

it's my folks," she whispered. "We mustn't let them see us!"

"Yes, I recognize the boat now," I whispered back. Then I laughed a little. "We can talk out loud. They can't hear us."

Clara didn't laugh, and I could see the furrows on her brow as she watched the opposite shore nervously.

I wondered how long the McCrumbs had been there and what was happening. I wondered how long they'd stay. What about the search party from Gull Harbor? Had they reached the Cliffs yet?

No sooner had the thought entered my head than I glimpsed a group of men coming down the path from our house to the wharf. Two of them broke away and slowly trekked along the shoreline, searching the few bushes that grew sparsely in the rocky soil. Others went in the other direction, and some still on the hillside turned and went back toward our house.

"A lot of people are lookin' for you, Clara." Despite myself, I still felt the need to whisper. "See how they're searching for you?"

"I hope they don't come out here after me." Clara moved closer to me and spoke in a hushed voice. "I wish they'd all go home."

I prayed silently that no one would think of coming out to Lonesome Isle.

Clara and I sat at the gull gaze, watching and waiting for the McCrumbs' boat to back out from our wharf and head to Gull Harbor. In the warm sun and salty wind, Clara's eyes began to close, until she finally put her head in my lap and slept. It was comforting to know she was not afeared and trusted me to keep her safe.

The wind whistled through the fir trees, and in the sky fish hawks soared in large circles, their wings stretched out and still. I watched them soar higher and higher until they became small dots against the blue sky.

A sudden, eerie wail startled me back to the real world. I heard it again, chilling my very bones and prickling my skin with gooseflesh. Never had I heard such a mournful cry—not even when Blizzard had howled the night of the storm. This was higher-pitched—more humanlike.

The wind was colder now and strong. The waves on the sea rose high and crashed on the shore behind me. The waters of the tickle turned darker. Then once again the ghostly wail rose from somewhere. Sad, pleading, pained.

The hollies! The stories were true! The wails of the shipwreck victims still cried out after all these years. The ghosts were howling, just as I had been told.

I heard it again. It seemed to come from the other side of the island, below the hill, near that place where the sea broke against the hidden rocks—where the steamer had lost its power and broken apart—where my grandfather's and uncles' broken bodies had washed up onto the shore.

I didn't move or make a sound, but stayed huddled and hidden with Clara among the bushes in the gull gaze.

CHAPTER 24

"The Hard and the Aisey"

After what seemed like hours the wind calmed, and the frightful sounds stopped. The sun was lower in the sky now, and shining on the Cliffs. My heart still beat fast and hard—and then I heard the faint sound of a boat engine. "It's Mom and Dad! They're coming home!" I cried out in relief, waking Clara.

"Will they come get us now?" she asked sleepily.

"As soon as the McCrumbs leave."

We watched our boat move slowly into the barrasway. Then Dad and Mom tied up behind the McCrumbs' boat.

Suddenly a man and a woman came rushing down the stairway to the dock. *Here we go,* I thought. *There's sure to be an uproar when Melloy McCrumb confronts Dad face-to-face.* But Dad would take care of everything. He'd calm everyone down. It was his way of dealing with things.

It wasn't long before the McCrumbs left. After

they had been gone for a while and Dad figured it was safe, he came to get us.

Clara and I had already gathered our things from the barn and were waiting eagerly on the old dock.

"Hop on board," Dad called as he glided carefully to the wharf. "Where's Raven?"

"In the barn," I told him.

"Erik and I will get her later."

I was just about ready to burst, wanting to tell him about the hollies, but not in front of Clara. That news would have to wait.

On the way home I asked Dad all about the visit from the McCrumbs. "Just wait until we get home!" he said over the noise of the engine. "I'll tell you all about it."

I tried again when we landed and were tying the boat to the grump heads. "You'll hear all about it," Dad said, concentrating on the knots. "Be patient."

"Patient? We've been on the island for hours wonderin' what's happenin'!" I grumbled under my breath. Dad gave me a look, so I grabbed Clara's hand and ran up the steps and onto the path leading home. Blizzard came running to us as we approached the house and jumped up to lick my face. "You blubbery kisser," I said, wiping my face with my sleeve.

It was getting dark, and the lanterns were lit. Flankers spat from the chimney and mingled in the darkening sky. Clara tried to keep up with me as I made a beeline to the kitchen door. "Mom's fired up the stove," I told her. "I'm starvin'—aren't you?"

I raced into the kitchen with Clara and Blizzard right behind me. "What did the McCrumbs say? Do they know we have Clara?" I demanded.

Mom was busy heating up a huge pan of pea soup. Gran cut up chunks of cooked ham and tossed them into the pot. Blizzard lay by the stove on his rug and looked pleadingly at Gran, who tossed him a piece of meat.

"Won't someone please tell me what happened today?" I begged.

Gran wiped her hands on her apron and sat down. "It was a right devilish afternoon, Jessie, let me tell. First the search party from Gull Harbor arrived, thinking Clara may be lost in the woods or drowned, and then—who should arrive but Henrietta and Melloy, as nasty as ever!"

Erik came into the kitchen and joined us at the table, straddling a chair. "They kept yellin' at me and

Gran, insisting we give up Clara. Before Mom and Dad came home, they demanded to know where we were hiding Clara. When we didn't answer, he went out into the barn. 'I'm gonna see if your horse is in the barn,'" Erik said, imitating Melloy's nasal voice. "'If she's not, I'll know that scamp granddaughter of yours took Clara off somewhere.'"

"What did he do when he saw Raven was gone?" I asked.

"He didn't think Raven *was* gone!" Erik laughed. "Melloy ups and checks out the barn, and there's that fairy horse I brought back, in Raven's stall, munchin' on hay as big as life. Melloy was thwarted, 'cause he figured it was Raven. The stupid bostoon! The horse is a *stallion*. Raven's a *mare*. He didn't know the difference!"

We all burst out laughing, and even Blizzard barked and wagged his tail.

"I was nervous as all get-out," Erik went on, "especially with Melloy carryin' that rifle around with him."

I gasped. "He had a rifle?"

Dad came into the house and was hanging up his jacket on a peg. "Yep, Melloy had a rifle—just to scare us, I'm sure."

"Well, he sure scared *me*," Mom said. "When we got home, there they were—quite a welcoming party, let me tell. As we pulled into the wharf, they came roaring down the steps to the dock with all kinds of accusations. They thought for sure they'd find Clara on board the boat, and when they saw we didn't have her . . ." Mom laughed. "Well, I wished I'd had a camera to show the expressions on their faces."

"As they left, they were threatening to send Chet Young, the Mountie, down on us," Dad added.

"Dad told them to go ahead and call the Mountie—that we had plenty to tell him about their cruelty and neglect of Clara," Erik put in. "Boy, did they shut up fast."

Dad went on. "Gran told us what the Doyles said—that Melloy gets a check every month from someone in Toronto paying for Clara's keep. I'm sure he's not tellin' whomsoever it is how Clara's gone missing. You can bet your bottom dollar he wants to keep gettin' that money." Dad turned to Clara. "Do you know of anyone in Toronto who might be a relative?"

She shook her head. "No one ever told me anything about money or relatives."

"Don Anderson's goin' to see what he can find out when he gets back to work in St. John's," Dad said.

"But in the meantime will the McCrumbs be watchin' for me, thinkin' I know where Clara is?" I asked.

"Perhaps they won't really care where Clara is, so long as they keeps gettin' that monthly check," Mom speculated.

"I warned Melloy McCrumb I'd be the one to call the Mounties if he came near our family," Dad said firmly.

I hoped that scared the McCrumbs out of our lives. I didn't relish the idea of being hounded by the McCrumbs—especially when Dad and Erik went away to the Labrador.

"By the way," Dad said, interrupting my thoughts, "while I was in Gull Harbor, I went up and took a look at that corral you told me about. Sure enough, there it was, just like you described it, Jessie, except there were nine horses fenced in there. Didn't you say there were four when you passed by?"

"One was missing—the one that's in our barn. So there should have been five when Clara and I were there."

"Well, he's got nine there now. I hear tell he's takin' them off the abandoned islands and bragging about his kindness."

Then I thought of Mike Hawley. "Dad! When you stopped at the Harbor, did you hear anything about Mike Hawley? Is he still alive?"

"I hear tell he's comin' along. But it may take a long time before he gets the use of that arm."

My heart sank. "Maybe he'd be all right if I hadn't chased him. Was it my fault, do you suppose?"

Dad shook his finger at me. "Get that thought right out of your head, Jessie. That boy was bound to get in trouble sooner or later."

Mom put her arm around me. "It was not your fault, Jessie."

"The Hawleys should forget about blamin' anyone and be thankful their little saucebox is alive and will recover," Gran stated.

"This will all blow over in time," Dad said. "You know that in life we have to take the hard and the aisey."

"Life is right hard. None of it is aisey!" I could feel angry tears welling up. "I never meant to hurt Mike, and now the Hawleys hate me. The McCrumbs hate me." My voice was rising. "I'll be afeared to leave the Cliffs ever again! And I'm afeared to stay here, too, especially when you and Erik have gone to the Labrador."

"Don't cry." Clara looked right worried and stroked my hand. "We'll both be safe here, Jessie. You'll take care of me, and I'll take care of you."

"Remember the good things you've done, Jessie," Mom said. "You saved Clara, and now she has a family who loves her."

"I'm goin' to put some flesh on you with good food, my child," Gran said to Clara. "You're so thin you could sleep on a clothesline."

"Sleep on a clothesline?" Clara burst out laughing. I realized it was the very first time I'd heard her laugh. "I'm goin' to stay here with my new family forever! You're my mother," she said to Mom. "You're my brother," she told Erik. "You're my dad," she said shyly to my father. She hugged me and said, "You're my real, true sister, Jessie.

"And *you* are my grandma!" To everyone's surprise Clara ran to Gran, threw her arms around her, and kissed her—smack!—right on the cheek!

That night while Gran and Clara did dishes, Mom and I went upstairs. I sat on her bed and said quite seriously, "Mom, something happened out at Lonesome Isle today that I haven't told anyone."

Mom looked startled, then sat next to me. "What happened, Jessie?"

"You know all the stories about the hollies, right?"

Mom smiled. "Of course, my child. Couldn't live around here without hearing those tales. Besides, Gran says the hollies were howling out there long before the big shipwreck."

"Have you gone out to island since the shipwreck? Have you ever heard them?"

"No! I'd never venture out to Lonesome Isle anymore. We must respect those who died in the shipwreck and leave them be with their mourning. Their lives were cut short, and now they're chained to Lonesome Isle." Then her expression turned to concern. "Did you see or hear anything strange out there?"

I nodded. "It's true, Mom. I heard them hollies, just as clear as I'm hearing you now. They howled—eerie, dreadful cries."

"Oh, my blessed savior!" Mom bit her lip. "Stay away from there, Jessie."

"So you believe me?"

"I know you wouldn't lie to me. Besides, all my life I've heard folks speak of tokens: death omens, sounds, and apparitions. And the people in Gull Harbor have seen lights where ships have gone down, and all sorts of weird things."

"Dad would say it was all pishogue, so don't tell him, Mom."

"I won't," Mom said. "Maybe you were ascared; bein' out there alone; you imagined the howling."

"I heard the hollies, Mom. I didn't imagine it."

"Leave them be, those hollies." She took my hands. "Jessie, don't go out there again, my child. Just leave the hollies be."

CHAPTER 25

"A Girl After Me Own Heart!"

Even though things stayed quiet for the next several weeks, I still had creepy feelings. Was someone from Gull Harbor watching us from the woods? From a passing boat? And each time I looked over at Lonesome Isle, I shuddered, remembering the hollies.

Uncle Don wrote to Dad a few times from St. John's. He was finding it hard to trace Clara's real family.

As you know, adoption laws are seldom enforced here. Can't find records of Clara's birth, baptism certificate, or any other legal documents yet. But I'm still checking other agencies, including the Grenfell Mission and church baptisms in Labrador.

Meanwhile Gran kept us busy setting the garden. In the winter Mom and I had started vegetables and flowers in boxes in the cellar, and green sprouts had already pushed up two or three inches or more from the soil.

After Erik plowed the earth in our plots, we planted our seedlings, potatoes, radishes, turnip, carrots, peas, and cabbage in neat rows. "Now that the days are gettin' so long, we'll be eatin' these before you know it," he said.

Blizzard was always by our side as we worked, his tail wagging, as if to make sure we were doing it right. Raven kept her eye on me, watching my every move from the fence. In the afternoon I'd ride her around bareback, sometimes with Clara hanging on behind me.

Erik picked up some of the fences that had fallen in the snow and set them up so the horses couldn't get into next winter's food. The new horse, especially, was used to running free, and so Blizzard and Raven chased after him, herding him away from the garden or from the cliffs around Devil's Head.

Clara had come to love the new horse, so we let her give him a name. For several days she thought about it and changed the name a dozen times before she was satisfied and settled on Cocoa.

Clara spent hours knitting and purling squares for a quilt that she was putting together to surprise Mom.

Gran was amazed at how quickly she learned. "Clara's easy to teach," Gran told me. "Not like you!"

"It's not my fault I'm left-handed. But it's *your* fault if you can't teach left-handed people how to knit!" I knew Gran was actually teasing me in her own strange way.

One day after the coastal steamer came in, Dad returned from Gull Harbor with a letter for me from Sandra. I had written her a couple of weeks before and told her all about Clara and what was going on with the horses here. Sandra answered me quickly.

Clara must be like a little sister to you. And since you told us her sizes, we'll include clothes and shoes for her in the next barrel we send.

Now that school is out, I ride horseback every day through the park reservation in Stoneham. I'm going to be working at the stables all summer. You said you have a new horse. It must be wonderful to own another Newfoundland pony. I've told all my friends about them and we all wish we had one. I feel so sad about all those ponies

being abandoned after all the good things
they've done for people. Isn't there some way
to help them?

I wondered this myself over and over, if there was
some way to help the ponies—especially those in
Melloy McCrumb's corral. What would happen to
them in Quebec? It couldn't be good—not with the
way everyone shut their mouths whenever I asked.

Erik, who had received a letter from Ned, interrupted my thoughts. "Ned's coming back to stay with
us once he's out of school. He said to tell you he
hopes the berries will be ripe."

"That will be nice," I said, trying not to appear
excited. "Does Ned know you may be going to the
Labrador with Dad?"

"Dad isn't sure he's going now." He sounded disappointed at first, but then he brightened up. "Since
Ned's comin', I'd rather be here anyways."

I ran to find my father, who was working on nets in
the barn. "Erik says you're not going to the Labrador.
That you'll be fishing close by. Is it true?"

Dad put his arm around my shoulder. "Yes, maid. I
was goin' to tell everyone at supper. I've decided with

things the way they are . . . well, I'll feel better stayin' closer to home this summer. I've talked to Pete Doyle and George Rideout. We've decided to set up our own little fishery in these local waters. We're dividin' up expenses."

"Dad, are you afeared of leavin' us alone? Has there been any talk or trouble at Gull Harbor with the McCrumbs?"

"Most everyone figures we've got Clara, but they know she's better off with us. Howsomever, the McCrumbs are venomous, and they may try somethin', knowin' them."

"What about Mike Hawley? Is he any better?"

"Ah, yes, my child. You'll be glad to know he's home and walkin' around. He wears a brace on his neck and a cast on his arm. They say he's quieted down since the accident. I haven't seen his folks, I'm glad to say. At some point I'm goin' to have a talk with the Hawleys. But right now, while Jack is thick as thieves with Melloy McCrumb, I'm stayin' away. The two of them are up to no good, I'm sure."

"So that *is* why you decided not to go to the Labrador. You're afeared for us."

"Not afeared. Just bein' cautious, Jessie."

"I guess I probably shouldn't go to Gull Harbor, right?"

"Why would you even think about goin' down there? We told you to stay away."

"Dad, I want so badly to see my friends," I said.

"You got Clara here as a friend, and Ned's comin' to visit."

I was about to leave the barn, and then I stopped. This was not fair! I saved Clara from a terrible home, and I never once touched Mike Hawley. So why was I hiding as if I'd done something wrong?

I turned around and went back to Dad. "I'm not goin' to hide anymore, Dad. Next time you go to Gull Harbor, I'm goin' with you. If anyone says anything to me about Clara, I'll tell them to mind their own business. And if the Hawleys say one word to me, I'll stand up for myself. Please take me when you go tomorrow. Please?"

At first Dad looked puzzled. "I'm not sure this is a good idea, Jessie."

"I'm sure. I haven't done anything wrong, so I'm free to do whatever I want."

"You'll need to be cautious, too," Dad said seriously. Then he grinned and put his arm around my shoulder. "Ah, maid, you're a girl after me own heart!"

CHAPTER 26

Real Bad News

Early on a Thursday morning, just before the tide turned, and despite Mom's protests, Dad and I started out for Gull Harbor. Blizzard came running down to the wharf with us, his tail shaking like a tree in a gale. "No, Blizzard, you need to stay home with Clara," I told him. He looked sad when we backed the boat out and left him standing on the dock.

The tide was going out, so the current was strong, but Stony Tickle was shallow. The sky was clear blue, and I was watching two eagles circling overhead, when Dad said, "Keep an eye out for rocks, Jessie."

I moved up to the bow and signaled right and left with my hands as we moved slowly through the sunkers and shoal water. I knew these rocks so well I even named them. One I called Giant because it was big and round, like the head of a giant. At high tide just the top appeared above the surface. At low tide the whole head jutted out of the water, like a giant watching for boats to trap.

The tricky thing about that huge boulder was that if anyone unfamiliar with the tickle were to be creeping through at low tide, he would likely steer away from the giant's head, only to be caught by the giant's hand—a jagged part of the same rock that was usually submerged.

Smaller sunkers that I'd named Old Hag, Scrape, and Jinker were equally dangerous.

"I could navigate this boat through here with my eyes closed," I bragged to Dad.

"It's different when you're driving the boat, maid, as I'm sure you know, since you took off by yourself that time." He grinned at me.

"Oh, Dad, I was mad when Erik made fun of me. I wasn't thinking. You should let me drive and I'll show you how good I am."

"Tomorrow–next day," Dad answered.

"That means never."

"No, it means *sometime*."

I was relieved to see no one was on the dock when we landed at Gull Harbor.

"I could use a cup of coffee at the bakery," Dad said. "How about you?"

We went inside and sat at the window overlooking the road. I ordered lemonade and a cold, creamy chocolate éclair. Dad had apple pie and ice cream with his coffee. *The last time I was here, Melloy McCrumb and Jack Hawley sat nearby,* I remembered nervously.

Mrs. Chase came over to our table. "Hello, Walt. And you too, Jessie. I haven't seen you for a while, my girl."

"No, I've been busy at the Cliffs," I answered. "June's for setting the garden, you know."

"You've had a lot goin' on up there, haven't you?"

"Well, if you mean the men from the shipwreck, they've gone back to St. John's," Dad said.

"No, I'm not talkin' about those gentles; I'm talkin' about Clara. Isn't she at your place?"

At her words my hand began to shake, and I tried desperately not to spill my lemonade. "Are you sayin' that Clara hasn't been found yet?" I asked innocently.

"Wherever that little girl is, I'm sure she's better off than with the McCrumbs," Mrs. Chase said, with a knowing wink at Dad.

"How's the Hawley boy? Is he still a rambunctious saucebox?" Dad asked her.

"No, he's calmed down since the accident. He can't

get into as much mischief now, since he was hurt so badly."

"Does his father still blame me?" I asked.

"Don't worry, Jessie. We all know it wasn't your fault. But Melloy McCrumb is some mad at your family. He's convinced you took Clara away. So he's probably got Jack Hawley stirred up against the Wheller family too, since Jack and Melloy are business partners now."

"What is this new business they're into?" Dad asked.

"The horses from the islands. They've got a plan to sell them to a company in Quebec," Mrs. Chase answered.

"What kind of company?" I persisted. Out of the corner of my eye I could see Dad shaking his head at Mrs. Chase as if to say, *Don't tell her.*

But Mrs. Chase didn't notice and continued. "Why, to the cannery up there. You must have heard by now. They're selling the horses for their meat."

CHAPTER 27

The Fate of the Horses

When I heard what Mrs. Chase said, I choked on my pastry. While I coughed and spit up crumbs, Mrs. Chase put her hand to her mouth and looked apologetically at Dad. "Oooh, I'm so sorry. Perhaps you hadn't told Jessie about this."

"They're bein' sold for their *meat*?" I exclaimed. "Who'd eat a pony? It's like eating Raven, or Blizzard! Tell me it's not true, Dad," I begged. But inside I knew that it was true and that that was why Dad and Mom were trying to keep it from me.

Mrs. Chase left our table and went to pour coffee for herself and Mrs. Tilley, who had come into the bakery. The two women sat down together at a nearby table.

Dad put his hand on my arm. "Shh, Jessie. Don't get so troubled."

I could hear Mrs. Chase whisper loudly to Mrs. Tilley, who was quite deaf, "Poor Jessie didn't know the horses were being sent off for horse meat. She's all upset. Most of the children haven't been told, and I had to open my big mouth."

"I don't think most of the adults knew Melloy was sellin' the ponies for . . . *that*," Mrs. Tilley whispered loudly.

I struggled to speak. "Why are those barnacles doing this?

"Money," Mrs. Chase answered from her table. "I don't imagine it's much, but Melloy and Jack are out for any money they can get."

"Who eats ponies, anyway?" I demanded again. "Those . . . cannibals in Canada?"

"Oh, Jessie, remember we are Canadians," Mrs. Chase said. "In any case the meat will be canned and sent to other countries, I think."

"Well, you know the old Newfoundland saying, Jessie: 'The death of a horse is the life of a crow,'" Mrs. Tilley said. "Think of it, my girl. The horses were out there on the islands fending for themselves. When winter comes next year, they'd die of starvation and be left for the crows. That would be worse."

"Why were they left on their own in the first place?" I demanded.

"It's expensive to keep a horse." Mrs. Chase said.

"Especially now, when we don't need them as much."

"Perhaps you've forgotten that our horse, Raven, helped save those shipwrecked men," I reminded them. "I suppose we should get rid of her, too."

"I know how you feel, Jessie, but how can we stop people from sending the horses off to Quebec?" Dad asked. "It's happening all over Newfoundland, not just here."

"We can at least stop it from happening to *our* ponies here in Gull Harbor. We can't let Melloy McCrumb round up horses in that corral only to be killed. We've got to do something!" Tears were spilling down my cheeks, and my nose was dripping. "When is it goin' to happen?"

"The wagon will be comin' here next Wednesday to pick up the horses," Mrs. Chase said.

"Next Wednesday?" I cried. "Today's Thursday. Wednesday's less than a week away!"

"It's the only day they'll be comin' this way," she explained. "After that they go to other parts of Newfoundland."

I could hardly speak I was sobbing so hard. Dad took my hand. "Shh, Jessie. We'll talk about it when we get home," he said quietly.

Mrs. Chase, Mrs. Tilley, and Dad tried to console me, but I didn't hear their words. My mind churned as their voices droned on. I knew I couldn't save all the ponies in our province, but there had to be some way to rescue the ones Melloy McCrumb had gathered into that corral.

"Look here, my girl." Dad pointed to the door. "You wanted to visit your friends, so go on now and visit them while you're here. You'll feel better then."

I slammed the door as I left the bakery without even saying good-bye. I couldn't stop the tears, but I was determined to find a way to save those horses. I needed to talk to Meta.

Since school was out for the summer, Meta was in the kitchen with her folks when I knocked on the door and went in. "Jessie!" she exclaimed, and ran to hug me.

"Come in, sit down, maid," her mother said, pulling out a chair. "Here. We have nice fresh Irish soda bread with plump raisins—still warm. Now don't make shy."

Uncle George Rideout was sipping tea and looking at a fishermen's magazine. "Good mornin', Jessie," he said. "Sit down and bide a while."

Even though I tried to listen, I hardly knew what

Uncle George was saying—something about the new fishery he and dad and the Doyles had planned for the summer.

Then Meta's mom eyed me funny-like and said, "Clara's still missin', you know. But we're convinced a kind family has taken her in."

"Most likely," I said with a nod. I still wouldn't say right out we had Clara, but I could tell they had figured it out when Meta and her folks smiled at each other.

When we were finally through with tea and gabbing, Meta and I sat on the back steps. Once outside, I asked her right away about the ponies in Melloy's corral. "Do you know what's goin' to happen to them?"

"No. I just heard that Melloy's goin' to sell them to someone from Quebec."

I took a deep breath and told her, word for word, what I had heard from Mrs. Chase. Meta put her hands to her mouth. "Does my pa know they're goin' to kill the ponies? If he allows that to happen . . . I'll never forgive him. Never!"

"Perhaps they don't know 'sactly what's goin' to happen. Or they don't want you to be sad. Melloy may have just told them the horses will have a better life in Quebec," I said.

"Isn't there somethin' we can do?" Meta asked.

"There may be a way to save the horses."

"How? I'd do anything, Jessie."

"Anything?" I asked. "Will you help me kidnap the horses?"

CHAPTER 28

My Secret Plan

Kidnap the horses?" Meta's eyes grew bigger and bigger as I explained my idea. "Do you think we could do it?"

"We can't do it by ourselves. That's why I've got to see the Doyle twins while I'm here. Maybe Brianna Briggs and Margie Rand will help too."

"Let's go tell the twins about this right now," Meta said eagerly.

We dashed over to the Doyles' house. Trudy and Polly were on the porch. "It's Meta and Jessie!" Polly shouted. She and her sister leaped off the steps and ran to us.

"Jessie, Meta! We got a telegram last night from our sister Judy in Corner Brook!" Trudy yelled. "She's had the baby! It's a boy."

"His name's Bryan," Polly said. "We have a little nephew. We're aunts!"

"Mom and Dad are Grandma and Grandpa," Trudy giggled. "Ain't this wonderful happy news?"

"It is, it is!" I said. Suddenly there was a long pause, and the twins noticed how serious Meta and I had become. They stopped their chatter and looked at us curiously. "I have a secret to tell you," I whispered. "But first you've got to promise you won't tell anyone."

"We won't tell. Honest, Jessie," Trudy said, while Polly nodded.

We sat on the steps, and I told them what Melloy McCrumb and Jack Hawley planned to do with the horses.

"Good morrow to you!" Polly exclaimed. "No such thing!"

"It's true," Meta said. "Now listen to Jessie's idea on how we might be able to save them."

"I'm thinkin' we could capture the horses before the wagon comes to get them," I said.

"Capture the horses?" Trudy looked stunned.

"When?" Polly asked.

"We'll have to do it before Wednesday, or it will be too late," I said. "That's when the wagon comes for them."

We sat and talked, and I told them my idea. Then Trudy shook her head. "It ain't possible for us to do this, Jessie."

"Gran always says that anything worthwhile is possible," I insisted. "And I think this is worthwhile. Don't you?"

Everyone nodded, and then Meta asked, "What will we do with the horses after we kidnap them?"

"We'll hide them for a while."

"Where?" Polly asked.

"Where no one would think to look."

"Tell us!" Meta demanded.

"We'll herd them out to Lonesome Isle."

"Lonesome Isle!" the twins yelled together.

"Go on with ya!" Meta cried out. "That place is haunted!"

"Jessie, your brain must be gettin' dim," Trudy said.

Polly nudged her sister. "Your heart's in the right place, Jessie. But we're not certain we can do it."

"For one thing, it's a long way to lead them all the way up to the Cliffs," Meta said. "We'd get caught."

"Not if we did it at night . . . in the dark," Polly suggested.

"Up the fairy path?" Trudy asked.

"Of course," her sister said. "That's the only way, unless we took them by boat. We can't take a dozen ponies in a boat by ourselves!"

"Still, Jessie, between us and all harm, how would we get out of the house in the middle of the night? What would we tell our folks?" Meta asked.

"That needs some workin' on," I agreed.

"What scares me the most is gettin' them out to Lonesome Isle," Polly said.

"We'd bring them out through the tickle," Meta said. "We could manage if it were between tides."

"I'm more scared of Lonesome Isle than the tickle!" Trudy exclaimed.

"See? That's why Lonesome Isle would be perfect," Meta said. "Everyone's scared of that place. No one would think we'd ever go out there in a million years."

"I went out to Lonesome Isle a few weeks ago," I told them.

"Did you hear the hollies?" they all asked at once.

My friends would never go with me if they knew I'd heard those awful cries. "It was nice out there— lots of grass and a big barn."

"Oh, Jessie, this is some complicated," Polly said uncertainly.

"But I wants to save the horses," Trudy argued.

"Exactly," Meta agreed. "It poisons me to think of those ponies bein' killed."

"We'll find a way. We've got time to think about it more," I said. "You might let Brianna and Margie know about our plan. But no one else, right?" I started down the steps. "I'll ask Dad to bring me back day after tomorrow—Saturday mornin'—after we all do some thinkin' on this."

"Okay," Trudy said. "Let's meet at the schoolyard."

Trudy nodded. "Meanwhiles we'll put our brains together here and see if we come up with ideas too."

"Remember, don't say a word to anyone. This has got to stay a secret."

"We promise," the twins said.

"I'll see you on Saturday mornin'—if Dad will bring me—and we'll work it all out." I left my three friends on the porch and headed back to the wharf. Dad wasn't there, so I looked around, wondering what to do with myself while I waited. I didn't like being alone so close to the McCrumbs' house.

Then I had an idea. I would answer Sandra's letter while I was near the post office. That way it would go off tomorrow instead of later.

Perhaps Dad was in there. The little bell on the door tinkled as I went inside. "Your dad left a while ago," Mr. Chase, the postmaster, told me. "He was goin' up to the Rideouts' lookin' for you."

Suddenly the bell on the door rang again. I turned around to see if Dad had come in. But there I was, face-to-face with Henrietta McCrumb!

CHAPTER 29

Confrontation with the Wicked Witch

Henrietta McCrumb's dark eyes narrowed when she saw me. "Well, well, look who has the nerve to show up in Gull Harbor! Jessie Wheller! Only you would be so brazen."

As she came toward me, I backed up, unable to speak.

"What's the matter? Cat got your tongue?"

"Good morrow, Mrs. McCrumb," I said, my voice shaking.

She came closer. "What have you done with my daughter?"

I bit my tongue so hard I could taste blood. "Clara's not your daughter."

She shook her finger in my face. "Where is she? I'll have the Mountie after you and your family, you little witch!"

Me, a witch? At this moment Mrs. McCrumb looked just like a wicked, ugly, evil witch herself. I suddenly lost all fear of the McCrumbs and took a step forward. "Yes, let's call the Mountie right now." I moved closer to the woman. "I'll be only too happy to tell Chet how you beat Clara and sent her to school without food." Now Mrs. McCrumb was backing away from *me*.

"Oh, dear, why don't you . . . perhaps you should go outside," said Mr. Chase from behind the counter. "Or . . . go get your dad, Jessie. Perhaps Henrietta should speak to him instead of you."

"No, I can speak for myself," I declared loudly.

I hadn't even heard the little bell on the door, but to my surprise Miss Campbell, the teacher, had entered the post office and heard the words between Henrietta McCrumb and me.

"I'll be only too happy to tell the Mountie how many days I gave Clara lunch because she had none," Miss Campbell said. "And while I'm at it, I'll mention the bruises I've seen on her body as well."

"Why, Irene. I'm shocked to hear such awful talk from you." Mrs. McCrumb put her hand to her breast. "My heart is broken. I adore Clara. She's like my own child."

"Your heart is broken?" Miss Campbell laughed.

"Oh, please, Henrietta. Everyone knows better. But the sad thing is that no one ever said or did anything to help Clara. If in fact Jessie *did* steal Clara away, I say *hooray* for Jessie—she's wiser and braver than anyone in Gull Harbor."

Henrietta McCrumb turned and headed to the door. "We will get our child back yet and the Whellers will be hearing from our lawyer," she said furiously. "You can be sure of that!"

CHAPTER 30

Moonstruck

"Are you all right, Jessie?" Miss Campbell asked, after Henrietta McCrumb had left.

"I'm fine, considerin'," I answered in a shaking voice.

Miss Campbell put her arm around my shoulders. "You are such a brave girl, to stand up to that woman."

"Thank you for standin' up *with* me," I said gratefully.

Mr. Chase looked concerned. "You folks better watch out for those McCrumbs. They're bad business."

Miss Campbell bought her stamps and left. "Take good care of yourself, Jessie."

I went to the counter where Mr. Chase was stamping mail. "Do you have plain paper that I can use? I have a letter to write while I'm waitin' for my dad."

"Here you go, maid." He pulled out a sheaf of paper and an envelope, then handed me a pen.

I wrote hastily to Sandra. I told her about the fate of our horses. I asked her to help us by telling everyone she knew how the horses were being slaughtered for horse meat. Then I begged her to ask around the stables where she rode: *If someone would care enough to adopt a pony or two, it would save their lives.* I ended by revealing that we were planning to kidnap the horses here in Gull Harbor.

I wrote Sandra's name and address on the envelope and bought enough stamps to mail my letter to Massachusetts. "When will she get this?" I asked Mr. Chase.

"Probably a week, since it will make tomorrow's steamer."

"Be sure it goes into the mail tomorrow, won't you? It's real important."

Mr. Chase grinned. "I'll be sure, Jessie." He took my letter and put it into a leather bag. "See? This whole bag's goin' onto the coastal steamer first thing in the mornin'."

"Thanks, Mr. Chase." I left the post office and scanned the road, hoping Henrietta McCrumb wasn't around. Dad wasn't back from the Rideouts' house, so I decided to take a walk up to the meadow and pasture where the horses were kept.

As I approached, they whinnied and ran to the side of the fence nearest me, shoving one another as if to say, *It's Jessie. She's come to get us out of here.* I noticed that all were wearing bridles.

The ponies were shades of brown with black manes. Some had white on their legs and on their faces. Several, like Raven, had soft white halos around their eyes. Some had the creamy ring on their muzzles that was known as mealy muzzle because it looked as if they had put their noses in a bucket of food and still had the mush on their mouths.

"You are a family," I told them softly. "You're all cousins from way back in ancient times."

Two ponies pushed each other out of the way to get my attention. I laughed as they scampered after each other and lined up, their heads over the top of the fence.

I held out blades of grass to them, which they took gently from my hand. One pony, who had a perfect white half-moon on her forehead, nudged my arm. I ran my fingers through her thick fur and mane. "You are a beauty," I crooned as she looked at me with her dark eyes. "If you were mine, I'd name you Moonstruck."

I put my arm around Moonstruck and lay my face against her soft neck. "We're goin' to get you away from here. I promise."

We've got to save them! We can't let anything happen to these sweet, lovable ponies.

CHAPTER 31

A Fight to the Finish

When I got back to the wharf, Dad was waiting. I told him about my row with Henrietta McCrumb. He nodded and patted my shoulder. "You handled yourself very well, Jessie. I'm right proud of you."

We headed out into the harbor, where swells lifted us gently and sunlight made the surface of the sea sparkle like millions of tiny crystals. A whale surfaced, then dove gracefully through the rolling waves off our starboard side.

The most peaceful place in my world was right here on the water. How I loved the sea. I couldn't imagine never seeing this awesome sight or hearing the *sish*ing sounds of the waves as the boat sliced through them.

The tide was still out, so once again as we entered Stony Tickle, I moved to the bow and signaled Dad right and left through the rocks.

Within an hour we were back at our wharf, tying up. Blizzard, who heard the engine, came running down to greet us, his tail wagging his whole body. As soon as I climbed out of the boat, he jumped up to lap my face. "Good boy," I said, rubbing his head.

Erik lumbered down the steps too. He said he'd been working on the garden all morning, as Dad had instructed him. "Any mail?" he asked.

"You got another letter from Ned," Dad said, handing it to him.

Erik tore it open, turned his back, and read it. "Yahoo!" he yelled, dancing around. "Ned's out of school. Dad, he's takin' you up on your offer for him to help out around here."

"I didn't know Dad had offered Ned a job," I said.

"Ned felt it was imposition to come unless he could help out," Dad explained.

"His train arrives in White Falls on Saturday afternoon, and he wants us to pick him up," Erik went on.

I could hardly wait to see Ned again, but I wouldn't show my excitement in front of my brother.

"We'll go get him," Dad agreed. "I have some business in White Falls anyway."

"Dad, I have to go to Gull Harbor in the morning on Saturday. I planned it with my friend-girls—somethin' important."

"Sure," Dad said. "We'll drop you off on our way."

We headed back to the house. In the kitchen Mom had tea brewing. Gran and Clara had made molasses cookies, and I giggled at the sight of Clara. Gran had tied an apron on her that came almost to the floor.

As the family sat together, I told them about my quarrel with Mrs. McCrumb. I noticed Clara twisting the edge of her apron. When I was finished, she grabbed my mother's hand and looked up at her anxiously.

"Don't worry, my child," Mom told her.

"We'll fight to the finish before we'll let you go back to those people," Dad promised.

It might very well be a fight to the finish, I thought, remembering Henrietta McCrumb's words: "The Whellers will be hearing from our lawyer. You can be sure of that!"

After tea I went out to the pasture and called Raven. She came eagerly, and I knew she wanted me to ride. So I climbed on her back, and we trotted around the grass and over by the big hill where the fairy path began. It was just Raven and me and the trees and wind. Then we clambered down to the beach, where I dismounted and walked along the sandy stretch.

When I came to a large boulder, I sat down and played ducks and drakes. As I sat there, skipping smooth rocks across the surface of the water, Raven nosed around the seaweed and the plants growing between the rocks.

I had a lot of thinking to do before meeting with my friends on Saturday. When I'd told the girls about my plan, I may have sounded as if I had everything in order to get the horses, but it wasn't really true. I hadn't even figured out a way to get out of the house myself late Tuesday night. Then there were the tides and bringing the horses out to the island.

Oh, my! I suddenly realized I really hadn't planned for everything that might go wrong. Perhaps I should forget the whole thing.

Then I recalled Moonstruck, with her mealy muzzle and those halos around her eyes that showed she was a descendent of the Exmoor horses from southern Wales. I thought about her soft nose nuzzling me.

At that moment my own pony, Raven, nestled up to me. I put my arm around her neck. "Knowing what I do, Raven, how could I do *nothing?*" I asked her.

She brushed against my shoulder with her nose, and I noticed the halos around her dark eyes. "You're one of those horses, girl," I said. "And you want me to save them, don't you?"

She nickered softly, as if to answer me.

I stood up and rubbed her ears. "Dad said we'd fight to the finish for Clara. Well, no matter what happens, I will fight to the finish to save those ponies."

CHAPTER 32

"We Can Do It! We Can Do It!"

Saturday came before you could say trapsticks, and I was so engrossed and nervous with the thought of what was ahead that I could hardly eat. Gran noticed. "What's wrong with you, Jessie? You've only had a tayscaun of food all day."

"I'm thinkin' about the ponies and what's goin' to happen to them next week," I said.

Gran sighed. "Let the men handle it. Stop thinkin' about it all the time. You'll go crazy, I swear. When you can't do anything about a problem, let the men handle it, is what I say."

"Gran, you always told me that nothin's impossible if it's worthwhile."

"That's true. But you're just a young girl who shouldn't be thinkin' about men's problems—just like you shouldn't drive a boat. Be a nice little girl, like Clara. We've had fun making cookies and soup and keepin' the house sparklin'."

I wasn't about to argue with Gran. She always won.

When I left on Saturday morning with Dad and Erik, no one asked what exactly I'd be doing in Gull Harbor. I guess they figured I was just going to visit my friends. I never shared my secret plan about the horses with anyone in the family.

Dad dropped me off at the wharf without tying up the boat or even turning off the engine.

"Too bad you can't come with us down to White Falls to welcome Ned," Erik said to me as I pushed the boat away from the dock.

"I wish I could, but I'll see Ned when you come back for me."

"I hope you'll be all right here until this afternoon, Jessie," Dad said. "Keep away from the McCrumbs. I may have a surprise when I come back."

I waved good-bye and ran up the stairs to the road. It was close to ten o'clock, so I went directly to the schoolyard, where Meta, Margie, and Brianna were waiting. "Where are Polly and Trudy?" I asked, fearful they might have dropped out.

"They're comin'," Meta said.

While we waited, I told them my plans, which now were in better shape. Margie and Brianna weren't sure about the whole idea, but I was able to answer most of the questions and put their fears to rest.

"How will we all get out?" Margie asked. "If my folks find me gone in the middle of the night, they'll set up an alarm that will be heard all over Newfoundland."

"I'm thinkin' of putting pillows under the covers to look like I'm there," Brianna said. She giggled. "You know what? This will be the most exciting night I'll ever have in my whole life!"

"I'm still tryin' to figure out how to get out of the Cliffs in time to meet you all at the corral," I told them.

At that moment Polly and Trudy came running down the road and into the yard. "I swear the good Lord is watchin' over us, Jessie. Guess what! Our folks are takin' the train to Corner Brook on Tuesday to see the new baby," Trudy announced breathlessly.

"So we're goin' to be alone by ourselves Tuesday night!" Polly added. "We won't have any trouble gettin' out."

"Mom says that we're almost fifteen, so they're trustin' us to stay home ourselves until they gets back on Friday."

"You're all set, then. But what about the rest of us?" Margie asked.

We were all silent for a while, thinking. Then I came up with an idea. "In the States, my cousin Sandra has what they call 'slumber parties.' They paint their nails and swap clothes and do each other's hair. Maybe you twins can ask your folks if you can have a slumber party Tuesday night. Then we'd all be together, and we could sneak out quietly."

Trudy nudged her sister. "Let's ask Mom! She loves to hear about fun things people do in the States."

Polly nodded. "And if we promise to be quiet and not get silly, she'll let us have a slumber party. I'll go bail for it."

"Let's ask her right now!" The twins took off toward their house in clouds of dust from the dry dirt road.

The rest of us waited impatiently, hoping that the Doyles would agree to a slumber party. If not, we'd still be in a hobble trying to come up with a solution for Tuesday night.

Soon the twins were racing back excitedly. "It's okay! Mom said it would be fine, if we promise not to make noise and to go to bed early," Trudy exclaimed.

"I think they're feelin' bad they're not takin' us to see the baby," Polly said. "We wanted to go, but they didn't have the money for all of us to take the train."

"So Mom's makin' it up to us by lettin' us have the slumber party!" Trudy did a little dance.

"Don't forget, Meta's mother's comin' in to check on us before we go to bed," Polly reminded her.

Meta put her hands together as if in prayer. "We'll put on our best manners and be so good all day that my mom will have no worry at all." Everyone giggled.

Brianna frowned. "We'll need to get back before dawn so it will look like we've been in bed all night."

"Right. When Melloy McCrumb discovers the horses are gone, we don't want anyone suspectin' we had anything to do with it, see," Margie agreed seriously.

"One good thing," Meta said. "The horses are far enough out in the meadow so no one will hear us at that time of night."

"And then we'll go right into the woods," Brianna said.

"The *dark* woods," Margie added gravely. "I've heard stories about fairies in those woods."

"Pishogue! Don't worry, Margie. I have two bright lights that we'll turn on once we get into the woods," I told her. "The path will be as bright as day."

Brianna nudged Margie mischievously. "That will scare the fairies away!"

Margie ignored her. "Don't anyone wear green," she said solemnly. "Fairies hate mortals who wear green."

Everyone nodded. "Even though it's pishogue, it won't hurt to be cautious," I agreed. "No one should wear green Tuesday night."

"Oh, I hope we can do this," said Margie nervously.

Trudy put her hands on her hips. "Repeat after me: We can do it! We can do it!"

"We can do it!" Margie repeated, and then we all joined in. "We can do it!"

"We won't let them take away our horses!" said Trudy.

We chanted after her: "We won't let them take away our horses!"

Meta reached for my hand. "Perhaps we should say a little prayer, too."

We gathered into a circle, holding hands, and bowed our heads.

Meta spoke fervently. "Dear Lord, please help us to save the horses."

"Please be with us on Tuesday night when we rescue them," Trudy prayed.

"Don't let me be ascared," Margie pleaded.

"Yes, make us brave," I agreed.

"And dear Lord, please don't let us get caught," Brianna added.

"Amen!" we all said together.

CHAPTER 33

Clara's Family

It was Erik who picked me up. I reached out and caught the bowline he threw to me as the boat glided toward the dock. "Where's Dad?"

"Surprise!" Erik said. "Take a look." He pointed to another boat a little way out in the harbor. Dad and Ned waved from a nice big fishing boat.

"Oh, that's the surprise Dad was talkin' about, eh? That big longboat?"

"That's one of the surprises," Erik replied. "Dad's been lookin' that boat over at White Falls ever since he brought the Andersons back weeks ago. It's got a right powerful engine."

"I sure hopes they catch enough fish to pay for it," I said.

"The Rideouts and Doyles pitched in with Dad, and it'll help out a lot with their new inshore fishery. The trap skiff will still be handy for around the harbor, but this is a forty-five-foot long-liner that sleeps four. It has a cookin' galley, too. Now we can sleep and cook on board, way out in the ocean."

"When are they goin' fishin'?" I asked.

"Dad's fired up to go real soon."

"I don't think Uncle Pete will be goin' right away, Erik. His daughter Judy had a baby, so he and Aunt Liz are goin' up to Corner Brook to visit them next week."

"That won't stop George Rideout and Dad from goin' out on the water. Hmm, maybe Ned and I'll go along too."

I was right happy when Ned waved to me from the new boat. I wondered what he and Erik would think if they knew we were about to save the horses.

Once back home, everyone came down to the wharf to admire the new white boat. It wasn't span-new—none of us could afford a new one—but it was clean and newly painted and varnished to a shine.

"It's a keen boat," Ned said, "with a nice, smooth-soundin' engine."

"We'll be usin' it next week when we goes out into the local waters," Dad said. "It's big enough to hold more than a few quintals of fish, you can be sure."

"And where will you be dryin' them?" Gran asked. "Will you fix up our old stages and flakes around here—where we used to dry the fish? Will we be usin' them again?"

"Sure we will," Erik said, giving Ned a slap on the back. "Ned will help, won't you?"

Ned grinned. "I figured you'd be puttin' me to work."

"You've got to work for your keep, me boy!" Dad said with a hoot of a laugh.

"Looks like all of us women will be makin' fish again," Mom said. "Cleanin' them and saltin' them and settin' them out on the flakes to dry."

"Aye," Gran nodded. "We'll have Clara snip off the heads and gut 'em." Clara, who stood nearby, made a face.

As we walked up to the house, I asked, "Was Ned the other surprise?"

"No, Ned *has* the surprise. He'll tell you all about it," Erik replied.

"Tell me now," I begged Ned. "Where is it?"

"In this suitcase," Ned said.

"Come on, show me. I can't wait."

"Nope, the whole family's got to be together when you hear this. Especially Clara." He smiled and winked at Erik.

"So Erik knows. And Dad knows. But you won't tell me," I grumbled. Both boys nodded, and I stomped off ahead of them.

Once we got home and settled down, Dad called everyone to the kitchen table. Ned, who sat next to Erik, held a thick white envelope in his hands. Clara sat on my lap. "Gran says it's a surprise," she whispered. "Do you know what it is, Jessie?"

"I have no idea."

Clara looked up at me, and I realized that those eyes which had once looked so hollow and empty, were now sparkling; her face was plump and rosy. "You are right pretty, Clara," I told her. "The McCrumbs wouldn't recognize you if you were under their noses!"

I tugged her braid playfully, remembering how she'd wanted Gran to plait her hair just like mine. Gran must have tried, but Clara's blond hair was too short, and little ends stuck out like bristles.

When everyone was seated, Dad said, "Ned has some shockin' good news from St. John's. You tell 'em, Ned."

Ned cleared his throat as if he were about to make a speech. "My dad, as he promised, investigated records to find information about you, Clara." He smiled at Clara, and I could feel her body tighten up in anticipation. "It took a lot of searching, because many records have not been kept well over the years in Newfoundland and Labrador. But after scouring ship records and baptism records—and, by the way, information about Melloy and Henrietta McCrumb— pieces of the puzzle have come together."

Mom leaned forward, her hands folded on the table. "Tell us!"

Ned opened the envelope, which contained several documents, and pulled one out. "This is your baptism certificate, Clara. It proves who you are and who your parents were. Your parents were Philip and Rebecca Cadigan."

Clara inhaled a little gasp.

Mom said, "Rebecca and Philip. What pretty names."

"And here's a photo of them by their tilt in the Labrador." Ned handed a yellowed photograph to Clara.

"Oh, look how young they were," I said, looking over her shoulder. The woman smiled shyly, her blond hair falling around her shoulders. The tall, lanky man with his arm around her looked as young as Erik. In the background was a tilt, one of the tents folks lived in along the Labrador coast.

Clara didn't speak. She simply stared at the picture, tracing the figures with her finger.

"See your mom's belly? You were tucked inside her in that picture," Gran said.

"That's my very own mom and my very own dad," Clara finally said. "My mom was real pretty, wasn't she?" She kissed the photo.

"She was beautiful," I agreed.

"My father said that other pictures and records were given to the McCrumbs when they took you from the orphanage," Ned said.

"I never saw any," Clara said. "Not one single picture."

"My father wrote a letter—to all of you, actually." Ned unfolded the letter and started to read:

"'Dear family: I was finally able to find a bit of information for Clara. Her parents were both born in the Labrador. Their names were Rebecca and Philip Cadigan. Their fathers worked for the mining company. However, by the time Philip and Rebecca got married, the mine had closed and their parents had died, so Philip and Rebecca moved closer to the Atlantic, where he worked for a fishery.

"'They lived in a tilt their first summer, but by the time fall came, Philip was critically ill with tuberculosis and Rebecca was expecting Clara.'" Ned looked up at Clara, who held the photo close to her heart. "Fortunately for you, Clara, the Grenfell hospital ship, the *Strathcona*, came and brought your mom and dad to the hospital at St. Anthony. I'm sorry to tell you, though, that your dad died shortly after arriving. He never got to see you. He's buried up there in St. Anthony."

Clara nodded and looked again at the photograph.

"Do we know what happened to Rebecca?" I asked Ned.

He went back to the letter: "'Rebecca lived long enough to have her baby, Clara, and to care for her until Clara was about two years old. Then Rebecca passed away too.'"

"What happened to Clara after that?" I asked.

"She was at the Grenfell Mission Orphanage until she was about three. That's when the McCrumbs took her," Ned told us.

We all began talking round the table, and Ned interrupted. "But listen to this!"

Everyone became silent as Ned held up a certificate. "This is a copy of the document which gives Melloy and Henrietta McCrumb custody over Clara, and it's signed by Joseph F. Cadigan, 'Great-uncle and only surviving relative of Clara Cadigan.'"

"So there *is* a surviving relative?" Mom asked.

Dad frowned. "This must be the person who is sending money to the McCrumbs."

"Why didn't he take Clara to live with him?" Gran asked.

"Because the man is eighty-four years old now, and in a nursing home in Toronto. But he sincerely cares about her and sends money every month—along with a short letter to Clara," Ned answered.

"I never got a letter," Clara said in a soft, serious voice.

"The McCrumbs never gave them to you," said Dad. "No surprise there."

Ned continued. "My father talked with Mr. Cadigan on the telephone. He was shocked when he heard how Clara was mistreated, and he has stopped payments to the McCrumbs. He sent this letter for Clara." Ned handed Clara an envelope. It was addressed to Clara Cadigan in a shaky hand.

"Read it, my child," Mom said. "It's from your own great-uncle."

"It's hard to read," Clara said, handing the letter to me. "Read it for us, Jessie."

My Dear Clara,

I was saddened when the Honorable Donald Anderson told me of the harm you have endured from the McCrumbs—the people I trusted to take care of you and to help you grow up to be a happy and healthy child.

Your own parents, Philip and Rebecca, were good, devoted, and hard-working folk who would have wanted only the very best for you. I promised Rebecca that I would be unwavering in caring for you. I hope I have not failed by placing you in the care of that wicked family.

The Honorable Mr. Anderson has told me what a sweet girl you are. He has assured me that he will not allow the McCrumbs to reclaim their custody. It is my wish for you to stay in the fine home where you are now, with the Whellers, if that is acceptable with them and with you. Mr. Anderson told me that he personally vouches for the honesty and loving concern

the Whellers have shown by giving you
refuge and love.
　　I'll continue to send along funds on a
monthly basis to help with your education
and good health.

Sincerely and affectionately,
Joseph Cadigan

There was another long silence in the room. And then an outcry of cheers!

"Clara! Did you hear? You can stay with us!" I cried.

"But what if the McCrumbs still fight for Clara?" Mom asked.

"They won't once they see this," Ned said, holding up an official-looking document with a gold seal on it.

"There's more?"

"This is a court order. It says that the McCrumbs must stay away from Clara, under penalty of the law. It declares that Clara is now in the custody of the Wheller family."

"Who had the power to do this?" Mom asked.

"We ain't got a lawyer," Erik said.

"Why does Mr. Cadigan call Uncle Don 'the honorable' Donald Anderson?" I inquired.

"Yes, who had the power to take Clara away from the McCrumbs?" Gran asked. She reached out and took the certificate with the gold seal from Ned, looked it over, then held it up. "Look and see whose name is on here!"

The document was signed:

Donald E. Anderson, Minister of Justice
Province of Newfoundland

"Oh my stars," Mom whispered. "Ned, your father is probably the most powerful man in all of Newfoundland."

CHAPTER 34

Clara's Gift to Me

It wasn't easy to convince Mom and Gran to let me go to a slumber party. They had never heard of such a thing and weren't at all happy about it. Finally I realized it was the word "party" that concerned them. So on Monday, when I was getting worried that I might not be able to go, I decided to play down the party part.

Soon as I brought up the subject, Gran and Mom were ready to argue.

"You'll be carryin' on a rumpus," Gran said. "Proper girls shouldn't be doin' things like stayin' at a party overnight."

"It's not a party. Honest it isn't," I said. "We're goin' to help the twins take care of the house while their folks are gone. It's only one night. Not the whole week. Besides, Aunt Annie Rideout is goin' to be checkin' on us all the time."

"You won't be doin' anything worthwhile at a silly party. Remember, when hands are idle, the roof leaks," Gran recited.

For a moment I was ready to give up the whole idea. Then Mom spoke up in my behalf.

"Jessie always uses her time wisely. And the girls are good girls. They'll probably read or clean the place for Auntie Liz when she comes home. Right, Jessie?"

"We *will*! Besides, my friends will be right hurt if I don't show up. It'll spoil everything."

Mom sighed. "Well, you don't have much time with other girls. I thinks it'll be all right—but just for one night, see. They'll have to make other arrangements for the rest of the week."

"Thanks, Mom!" I kissed her and ran upstairs to pack up the things I'd need in Mom's suitcase.

I could hear Gran protesting to Mom. "Jessie is very impulsive. You never know what she'll do. Well, it's your decision, but don't blame me when . . ."

I missed out on the last words, but it didn't matter. Things were falling into place. I was going to save the ponies!

Clara came and sat on the bed watching me. "I hope you'll be safe in Gull Harbor," she said. "I never want to go there again."

"Melloy McCrumb can't come near you now. If he does, he'll be arrested. Uncle Don is about the most important person in all of Newfoundland—well, next to the Premier."

"I still don't want to go near Gull Harbor."

"I wouldn't want to go if I were you, either. But you don't have to worry anymore. We have the Government of Newfoundland on our side." I had already packed the rope leads for the horses in the bottom of the bag, and had hidden them with my sweater and pajamas. I threw a few pairs of socks into the bag, along with my boots.

"Will you need boots?"

"You never know," I replied.

I'd need them on the mucky fairy path. Hopefully the brook in the woods was all dried up since the day Clara and I went through.

"I will miss you," Clara said. She got off the bed and went to a little box that Gran had given her for small, special things. "I have a surprise." She held something behind her back. "I made it just for you. Close your eyes."

I did as I was told, and I felt Clara's arms around my neck. "Now look. It's a good-luck necklace. See?" She pointed to a small, smooth stone with a hole through it where yarn had been laced to make a necklace.

"That's a real fairy stone. I found it on the beach."

"And now the fairies will protect me?"

"Uh-huh. I wish it had a gold chain, but I crocheted the necklace with a chain stitch. Gran showed me how."

"Thank you, Clara. This is the most beautiful, special present I've ever had," I said, kissing her cheek.

And I would need all the luck I could get—even from the fairies, I thought.

CHAPTER 35

Midnight on the Fairy Path

It was early Tuesday when Pa brought Blizzard and me to Gull Harbor in the new boat. Dad tied up at the dock, where Uncle George was already waiting with nets and traps.

"I may not be back home until real late," Dad told me. "In fact, we may sleep out in the boat if we find the fishing's good. So I'll tell Erik and Ned to pick you up tomorrow in the other boat."

I didn't respond, 'cause I wasn't sure just where I'd be tomorrow. I was getting more ascared by the minute. At the same time I could hardly wait for night to come.

The Doyles—Uncle Pete and Auntie Liz—left about noon by boat for White Falls, where they'd get the train to Corner Brook. My friend-girls and I waved good-bye from the wharf and then went back to their house, where we cleaned up the dishes and then played with Blizzard in the backyard.

The rest of the day dragged on and on. Whenever

we talked about what we'd be doing that night, we all went from scared to brave, cheerful to gloomy, excited to angry, and then back again—one emotion after another all day long.

Later, other kids came by and talked about the big truck that was coming to get the ponies in the morning.

The sun was still shining at seven o'clock when Meta's mother, Aunt Annie, came over to make sure we were eating a proper supper and would wash up the dishes. She kissed all of us and before leaving she said, "If you need anything, come down to our house. But I hope you won't come and wake us up unless it's important. Remember, if this is what they call a *slumber* party, then that's what you'll do—you'll slumber, not make a rumpus!"

We all laughed and promised to be quiet, then said good night as she went out the door.

The time dragged by as we waited for darkness, which came late during Newfoundland summers. By ten o'clock the sky grew dim, and we began to light lanterns.

"When do we go?" Meta asked. "I don't think it will ever get dark enough."

"We should wait until eleven. It'll be dark by then,

and most everyone will be in bed," Brianna suggested.

"I'll turn out the lanterns now so Aunt Annie will see the house is dark and think we've gone to bed," Polly said. She snuffed out all the lamps, and then we sat around doing nothing. Just waiting and waiting.

Finally, I couldn't stand it another minute. "Let's get ready and go." I turned on my flashlight.

"Isn't it too early?" Meta asked. "Someone might see us."

"No! We've got to get going while we have the nerve," Brianna said.

"By the time we're dressed, it won't be too early," I added.

It was close to eleven when I looked outside. Blizzard was sleeping on the porch. In the bright moonlight I could see him lift up his head and wag his tail as I peeked out the door. "Most of the houses are dark."

"Do you all have everything?" Polly asked.

"Yes," came the response.

"Don't forget to fill your pockets with treats for the ponies. They may need to be coaxed," Brianna reminded us.

"I'm ready. Let's go, before I change my mind." In the moonlight that drifted through the window, I could see Margie pale and shaking. Would she change her mind? Would she panic?

Meta stepped out onto the porch where Blizzard was sleeping. "We need to stay in the shadows," she whispered. "The moon is as bright as daylight."

"We can't make a sound. I hope none of you have noisy, scroopy boots," I warned as we began our walk. "Come along, Blizzard. We'll need you, too." Blizzard got up and followed us down the road.

The Rideouts' house was dark as we tiptoed by. "My folks always go to bed around ten," Meta whispered.

A light still glimmered as we passed the last house before the path to the meadow. Suddenly a dog barked, and a door opened. I grabbed Blizzard by the collar and held him close for fear he might bark or go after the other dog. We all stood totally still, hardly daring to breathe.

Someone in the house yelled, "Shut up, Ralphie!" The dog barked again. "Oh, come on in here," the voice said. "You make too much noise." After a final woof the dog went inside and the door shut, and after a moment that light went out.

We moved on beyond the store, post office, bakery, and telegraph office, then paused for a moment as we came to the McCrumbs' house across the street. After seeing no signs of anyone, we headed up the long dirt road toward the corral, where the horses were waiting.

When we arrived, we could see the ponies standing quietly, silhouetted in the moonlight. Three hovered together by the fence; others grazed. As we got closer, we could see a couple of horses lying on their sides, but as we approached, they jumped up and came toward us, whinnying softly.

I could hardly bear the thought of these sweet ponies being carted away in the morning to be killed!

Meta put her arms around one of the ponies. "Oh, this is the one I knew when we lived on Stepping Stone!" The pony responded by rubbing her nose on Meta's shoulder.

Trudy opened the bag she had brought and fed dried apple slices to another horse.

"Let's get them and go!" I said. As I peered into the moonlit corral, I could see that they all had their bridles on. "All we needs to do is hitch up the rope leads to each horse."

We lined up at the gate. "We'll go in one at a time, just as quiet as can be. We don't want them to get spooked." I lifted the latch on the gate and opened it just wide enough for me to slip inside the corral. The horses were curious, but not excited. These were all gentle, tame animals that were used to people. I slipped the leads onto two of the horses. The third didn't want it and pulled away. I just waited and talked softly, feeding him a carrot as I stroked him. Then, as sweet as could be, he allowed me to tether him. I tied those three ponies up to the fence post.

I petted the pretty little one I had named Moonstruck and gave her a slice of apple and a sugar cube from my pocket. As she nibbled daintily, I tied a rope onto her bridle and then hitched the other end onto a fence post. I went to another pony, and as I fed this one, two more came over and pushed their noses to my hand for bits of carrot that I held out.

The girls entered slowly, so as not to frighten the other horses. There were eleven horses in all. Cocoa would have made a dozen.

Before long we had leads attached to all the horses. We led the ponies out of the corral in pairs—cautiously, for fear they might jump or run. Amazingly, they seemed to remember their prior lives and came out easily—except for the two mares that Brianna was leading, which wanted to bite each other.

"Separate them," Meta ordered. "Swap with me." She and Brianna swapped one horse each.

"I'll stay last in line," Brianna said, "so they won't go after each other."

"Okay, Meta, you come behind me," I said. "I'm only taking one horse, because I'll lead the way with the flashlight. Blizzard will help keep the horses in line."

We walked in a row, leading our horses into the woods. It had been early spring when Clara and I had passed through, and the trees had been bare. Now the branches, thick with leaves, blocked out the stars and the moonlight. Once we were far enough into the deeper woods, I turned on the flashlight. When the beam of light lit up the woods and cast eerie shadows on the path ahead, Moonstruck stopped and reared as if seeing a new strange world. She whinnied, and the other ponies did the same, pulling against their rope tethers.

"Everyone stop!" I called out. "We need to quiet them. Maybe a piece of sugar might calm them down. Let's just stop until they get used to the light."

Blizzard circled all the horses, herding them in place. "Good dog," I said, petting him when he came back to me.

Once the horses quieted down, we moved on. The only sounds were the whooshing of the ponies' breathing, the clicking of their hooves over the stony trail, and the beating of our own hearts.

CHAPTER 36

Finding Our Way

Our trek along the fairy path seemed endless. I flashed the light ahead, and the only scene before us was the winding pathway, with more trees and darkness beyond. It hadn't seemed as long when Clara and I made the trip several weeks ago, and for a while I began to wonder if the fairies had changed the path and were leading us astray, as in many of the old folk tales.

The ponies were sweet and easy to control. Once or twice there was a squabble—some snapping or pulling against the leads. But on the whole they were docile and trusting.

"How much longer, Jessie?" Meta called.

"What time is it?" Polly asked.

We paused, and I looked at my watch. "It's half past one."

"It was a little after eleven thirty when we began the walk," Trudy said. "So we must be coming to something soon. Didn't you say there was a brook, Jessie?"

"Yes. But that was in the spring, after rain and melting snow. It may be dried up by now."

"Things always look different in the dark," Meta said. "It can't be much farther."

At that moment a wild screech cut through the night air, and the horses pulled on their leads and whinnied.

"Oh, my blessed fortunes!" Margie screamed. "It's the old nightmare hag—or maybe a ghost! I want to go back!"

"Stop it!" I snapped. "It's only an owl."

"This fairy path never ends." Margie began to cry. "It's scary."

"Don't be a grumbler and spoil everything!" I lashed out.

"I came all this way, and I'm kegged out, and . . . you . . . you are a bullamarue, Jessie Wheller!" Margie wailed.

"You *are* bein' mean, Jessie," Meta agreed. "Don't be so cruel to poor Margie."

Margie was still crying, and Brianna spoke up. "Hush, my girl. We're almost to Jessie's. This will be all over soon, so don't cry."

"You've been real brave, Margie," Trudy said gently.

"We haven't come across any brook yet," Margie whined. "I think we're lost."

"No, we're not," I said. "We'll be there any minute now."

We stopped for a while and stroked the horses. I felt for the fairy stone Clara had given me. It was comforting to know that it still hung around my neck. I reached for it and rubbed it—even though I knew the talk of fairies was a lot of pishogue. But we were on the fairy path, and if there were fairies to help us . . . *well let them come*, I thought.

Brianna passed us each a sugar cube, and instead of feeding them to the ponies we ate them ourselves.

I felt real bad. All my friend-girls had helped me with this idea, which was probably witless—and then I ups and yells at poor Margie.

Margie sniffled and stopped crying, but I heard her mutter, "Jessie's pure mean."

I went over and put my arms around her. "I'm right sorry, Margie," I said. "I shouldn't have yapped at you. You have been brave and uncomplainin', and . . . well, that owl scared me for a second too, and . . . I'm sorry." Margie just nodded. "Don't cry anymore," I went on. "Think on it. You are a hero—or whatever it is for girls?"

"Heroine," Meta answered. "We're all heroines for saving these horses."

"We're heroines. And we're almost to the Cliffs," I said.

"I'm so thirsty," Margie said. "I wish we'd brought water."

"Once we get to my place, we'll get a drink," I promised.

We'd gone another hundred yards or so, and I was beginning to worry if there was another branch of the path that we had mistakenly taken. What if we were lost? *I mustn't even think such a thing,* I told myself. *I mustn't let the others know I'm troubled.*

Just then, as we rounded a bend in the path, the beam from the flashlight fell upon the brook. "Here's the stream!" I yelled, standing aside and waving the light on the water so the others could see. "And just beyond that hill on the other side . . . is the Cliffs!"

Everyone cheered, softly of course, as we went to cross the little stream. The water was running, but gently. We were glad we wore boots. Before crossing the brook, each pony stopped and drank from the stream. "Good, sweet girl," I said to Moonstruck, patting her neck.

"What wonderful, clever horses," Meta said. All the girls agreed, and even Margie seemed less nervous, knowing we'd soon be out of the woods.

The horses made their way cautiously across the brook—as if checking each step for slippery rocks—and then clambered up on the other side. But then poor Margie slipped with a splash and fell into the water.

"Are you hurt, Margie?" I called, flashing the light in her direction. She'd gone headlong into the stream, and she came up dripping wet.

"I'm scraped and soakin'." I could tell by her voice that she was almost in tears again. "And I let go of the horses. They've gone ahead of me. Where are they?"

I flashed the beam up and down the side of the stream, where Margie's two ponies were quietly waiting. "Look! They're standing as good as can be waiting for you."

"They know you're in charge of them," Brianna added. "They wouldn't even think of running off without you."

I took hold of her horses' tethers while she wrung out her sweater and the legs of her pants.

"All we need to do is get over this little hill, and we

can bring the horses to our barn for now, see?" I said. "We can get warm and dry off and see what we need to do next."

We already knew our next step was to get the ponies out onto Lonesome Isle. But first the horses needed to rest, and so did we. I flashed the light on my watch. Two o'clock. If we rested, it would be almost three o'clock before we even started to take the horses across.

Would it be possible to get them safely over to the island before sunrise? And would the tide be in or out? Would the horses swim across? Should we lead them or ride them? I hadn't thought this all out, but we'd cross that bridge when we got to it—only how I wished there really *were* a bridge!

CHAPTER 37

Discovered!

We almost did a jig when we reached the crest of the hill and looked down at my home. The moon had fallen into the western sky and cast its soft, sleepy beams across the meadow below. There wasn't a single light on in my house. Everything was still and dreamlike in the moonlight.

"Let's go directly to the barn," I whispered, hoping the sound of hooves at this hour of the night wouldn't wake anyone. The few sheep we had were curled up sleeping in the pasture and never looked up. We made our way to the fenced-in area beside the barn. We gathered the ponies inside, closed the gate, and went into the barn. I pumped icy well water into a cup and passed it around.

Raven snorted, and in the next stall Cocoa stood up and pawed the floor of his booth. Both watched us curiously.

"Now it's time to think about gettin' those ponies over to Lonesome Isle," Trudy said.

"Is the tide out?" Meta asked.

"I'll take a walk down to see," I said. "The rest of you wait here." It was a short easy walk down to the beach. The water was dark, with only a few ripples that glistened under the moonlight, and it was shallow. The tide was out!

I ran back to the barn. "We should go now, while the tide's out," I said to the girls. "Can you do it? It shouldn't be much harder than the stream—except it's a longer way to get across."

"What about dry clothes?" Margie asked. "I'm frosty as an iceberg, Jessie."

"Okay, I'll get some warm clothes from my room."

"Bring sweaters," Brianna said. "Dry pants will only get wet again."

Blizzard wanted to go into the house with me, but I closed the barn door quickly so he couldn't get out. Before Clara had moved in with us, we had always left the house unlocked. But lately Dad locked the doors at night. The key was on top of the kitchen door lintel, and I turned it softly in the lock. I tiptoed into the kitchen and up the stairs, grateful for the moonlight shining through the windows.

Creak! I had forgotten that the sixth step always

made a squeak, so I stopped, waiting for any sounds from the bedrooms. After a moment I continued up the stairs to my room at the end of the hall. The door to my folks' room was shut, as was Gran's; so was the door to my bedroom, where Clara slept. But when I came to my brother's room, I could see the door was wide open. I held my breath and took one slow step at a time as I passed.

Erik and Ned were snoring loudly. At least the sounds would cover any noise I might make. I opened the door to my room cautiously and stepped inside. After grabbing sweaters and jackets from my closet, I headed out into the hall again with my arms full.

I moved even more slowly as I tiptoed down the stairs—forgetting yet again the noisy step, which squeaked even more loudly this time. I didn't stop to see if anyone woke up. Instead I dashed out of the kitchen and closed the door behind me.

Inside the barn my friends were waiting in the darkness. "It's me!" I said. Immediately Meta turned on the flashlight. "I have sweaters and jackets. Put 'em on quick before the tide turns. We've got a job to do."

Trudy put her fingers to her lips and pointed to

Margie and Brianna, who had curled up on a pile of hay and were sound asleep. "Oh, no," I wailed. "I know you're all tired, but we've got to finish what we started—before the sunrise."

"Wake up!" Meta said, shaking Brianna. "It's time to get the horses across the tickle. Don't quit on us now."

Brianna stirred and then sat up. "We're comin', we're comin'," she said in a sleepy voice. She looked down at Margie. "Come on, Margie. Get up."

"Oh, no—I was dreamin' I was home," Margie groaned.

"Let's get goin'. We can only take one horse at a time through the tickle. It will be too hard to manage two ponies if the current changes," I told them.

We went out into the night air once again. The horses were quiet. Two were lying down inside the fence. The others were munching on grass or drinking loudly from the watering trough.

I hitched Moonstruck to the tether once again, and the others did the same, only this time with just one horse apiece.

Could we bring the horses out there and still get back to Gull Harbor by sunrise?

We led the ponies out of the pasture and toward the beach, when I heard sounds. Voices whispering? Footsteps? A twig snapping?

I swung around and froze. Two dark forms crouched in the shadows, watching us!

CHAPTER 38

March to Lonesome Isle

With shaking hands I turned the bright beam of my flashlight onto the two figures. Erik and Ned were croodled by a tree, peering out at us with their mouths open, their eyes wide, and a look of pure astonishment on their faces.

"Is that you, Jessie?" Erik called. "I can't see with that light in my face."

"Of course it's me, you omaloor!" I yelled. "Who'd you think it was?"

The boys stood up, and I smothered a laugh. They were both in their pajamas. Aha! They must have heard me on that squeaky step and come out to investigate.

"Who's with you?" Ned asked.

The girls had stopped their trek to the water with the horses.

"It's me and my sister Trudy," Polly answered.

"And Meta, Brianna, and Margie," I added. "We walked from Gull Harbor."

"In the dark?" Ned shook his head in disbelief.

"Aye, and we brought eleven horses with us." Meta added.

"Let me get this straight. You *stole* eleven horses?" Erik had his hands on his hips.

"We didn't *steal* them. We *rescued* them," I snapped.

"Good morrow to you!" he sputtered.

"Someone had to do it, or they'd have been killed and sold as horse meat!" I was getting irritated. "We did this all by ourselves, but now that you and Ned are here, you can give us a hand." I crossed my arms over my chest and waited for their answer. "So, are you goin' to stand there like you're stunned, or are you goin' to help us?"

"What are you doin' now?" Ned asked.

"We're hidin' these ponies out on Lonesome Isle, since no one ever goes out there."

The boys still stood with their mouths open. I went over to Erik and punched him in the arm. "Come on, Erik. Help us hide the horses. We girls have already done most of the work."

Brianna called from the shoreline. "Never mind them. Let's get the job done. I'm takin' this horse, and I'm headin' out to Lonesome Isle right now. Is anyone else comin'?" I flashed the light on her and saw she was already up to her knees in the water. The other girls started into the water with their horses.

"We've got to get back to Gull Harbor before sunrise!" Meta yelled. "Are you goin' to stand there and wait for daylight, Jessie?"

"I'm comin'!" I turned to my brother. "If you tell anyone what we've done, Erik, I will never forgive you!"

I led Moonstruck down to the beach and followed the others out into the water. We'd reached the last part of our rescue journey—the march to Lonesome Isle.

CHAPTER 39

Changing Tide

We headed out into the cold water, leading our horses. The ponies were so tame that even when they hesitated, it didn't take much coaxing to persuade them to go on.

"Good girl," I said in a tender tone to Moonstruck. Even though I didn't know the pony's real name, she always responded to my tone. We moved on in a line. Meta had the other flashlight, and it glistened on the water. Ahead of me the girls with their horses were silhouetted against the setting moon.

The only sounds were the *splish-splash* of our wading steps and the occasional neigh or snort of the ponies. We were about halfway there and out into the full course of the tickle when I felt a slight dragging motion of the water and saw small churning whirlpools.

"Walk faster!" I called out. "The tide is turning."

The girls sweet-talked the horses and pulled on their leads. My pony tugged against me and snapped her head. "Come on, girl," I coaxed.

"Giddap, nan, nan, nanny!" Polly sang out the call for sheep but her horse responded. "Come on, nanny nan."

The water became shallow as we approached Lonesome Isle. "We're there!" Meta called.

Once on level ground the horses stopped, shook themselves, and waited, as if to say, *Now what?*

"Bring them into the barn," I said. "They'll get warm inside. We've got the rest of the herd to get."

The big barn door squeaked as we pulled it open, and we led the horses inside. "There are enough stalls for them all," I said, casting the beam of my flashlight around.

Once the six horses were inside, we closed the half doors that barred the stalls. I smiled as six heads peeked out over the tops.

"Is there water?" Trudy asked.

"I'll pump up the well when we get back," I told them. "Right now we've got to move quickly before the tide changes." I didn't want to sound afeared, but I knew how strong the current could be when the tide was turning.

We shut the barn door and raced back to the water. "I am so tired," Brianna said. "I don't know if I can come back here again."

"Don't think about it now," I said.

"Hurry—let's get back to Jessie's right away." Meta knew the danger of the strong incoming tide, since she and her father had been caught in the tickle once when they were out in a small punt.

We struggled through the water, which was now churning and circling the rocks and sweeping around our legs. "Let's all hold hands!" I yelled. The girls lined up behind me. Meta was at the rear with the other light, and I was in the front with my light. Margie held my other hand, clasping so tight her nails dug into my palm.

"We can do it!" Brianna sang out. "Say it! We can do it! We can do it!"

The rest of us mimicked her, but without much zest. We slipped and stumbled our way through the rising tide, which brought the cold water up to our chests when we reached the deepest part. "I can't swim!" Margie wailed.

"Well, neither can I," Brianna replied in a loud voice. "As long as our feet are on the bottom and our heads are above the water, we'll be fine." I knew Brianna was trying to be brave for everyone, especially Margie, who was starting to cry.

"Keep going. A little bit farther and it gets shoal again." I was struggling with the current and trying not to show my own fears. What if one of my friends drowned out here tonight? I lived on the sea and knew of many deaths from drowning.

Lord, forgive me for being so reckless, I prayed. *Please get us back safely.*

CHAPTER 40

More Horses to Go

Thanks be to the Lord," I whispered when we were once more in shallow water. Back at the beach Erik and Ned were waiting anxiously.

Margie was crying again, and we were all freezing and tired. The eastern horizon was just beginning to lighten. "There are still six more horses to go. Come on, we've got to get them out there."

"Not now, Jessie. You know it's too dangerous." Ned turned to Erik. "Why don't you take the girls back to the Harbor before sunrise?"

"Good idea," Erik agreed. "When I gets back, we'll help Jessie move the rest of the ponies to the island."

Relief swept over me. "That would be right wonderful, Ned. No one would suspect we spent the night kidnappin' the horses. Not when the girls are all asleep in their beds."

"No one would believe any of this," Erik said, shaking his head. "I still think I'm dreamin'."

My friends were huddled together up the path a

way. When I told them they were going home, they jumped up and down and hugged each other. They'd had enough of the whole scheme. "You may get back by dawn if you leave right now," I told them.

"What about you, Jessie?" Erik asked. "Won't they wonder why you're gone? You were supposed to be spendin' the night in Gull Harbor."

"Dad said you'd pick me up early this mornin', so . . . that's what the girls will say if anyone asks where I am."

"But it's still dark on the water."

Was Erik unsure about driving the boat? "The tide's comin' in, Erik. It will be hard to see the rocks. Why don't I drive the boat through the tickle?"

"No, I'll drive the boat." He still looked doubtful. "I . . . I'm just not sure where those sunkers are out there. Why don't you come and signal like you do for Dad."

"All right. You go start up the engine and check for gas while we get ready to leave."

Erik was already on his way to the boat.

"I'll hide the rest of the horses in the stable," Ned offered. "Better bring Blizzard. Isn't he supposed to be in Gull Harbor with you?"

"He's beat out," I said. "Keep him in the barn with

the horses, Ned. And don't let Gran or Mom or Clara anywhere near the stable, whatever you do."

I went back to the barn, grabbed some horse blankets, and then ran down to the boat, which Erik already had warmed up and running.

"Be careful out there," Ned warned as he pushed us out. "It's hard enough to navigate in the daylight."

The girls were snuggled up under horse blankets in the bottom of the boat as we backed out. I wrapped up in a blanket too and propped myself on the bow. "You direct me, Jessie," Erik said. "I'm countin' on you."

Although I always bragged that I knew every rock, I was right nervous now, as we slowly made our way through Stony Tickle. The water was dark, but with the bright beam of my flashlight I could just see the top of Giant's head. The other rocks were already submerged with the changing tide. I peered below the murky surface where the giant's craggy hand reached up toward us. "Turn port, quick!" Erik swung the boat away just in time.

I continued signaling with the light to the right and to the left as we crept between the other rocks, and I gave a sigh of relief when we came out of the tickle without a scrape to the boat or the propeller.

The pale light of dawn had already spread over Gull Harbor as we pulled in to the wharf. The horizon, though, was a deep red—signs of a coming storm. Perhaps that was why there were neither fishermen nor other early morning sights or sounds. The McCrumbs' house, like others, was dark, although it was still early enough that windows would show lights if folks were up and about.

"Out you go!" Erik whispered to the girls, who had been asleep. They untangled themselves from the blankets and clambered onto the wharf.

"Bye, Jessie," Brianna whispered. "I'll remember this night for a long time."

Margie took off my jacket and handed it to me. "I'm sorry I was such a crybaby, Jessie."

"You were brave," I said. "And we couldn't have done it without you, Margie."

"Bye, Jessie," Meta said, giving me a kiss. They all raced up the steps of the wharf and headed for the Doyles' house.

By the time we got back to the Cliffs, the tide had changed completely, so not even the giant's head was visible. Once again I leaned over the bow searching for the sunkers below the surface.

It became easier as the daylight crept over the calm waters.

"What a night this has been," I said as Erik brought the boat smoothly into our safe harbor.

He grinned at me. "And you are one amazin' little sister, Jessie."

CHAPTER 41

"Little Ponies, Follow Me, Follow Me"

Ned came running down to meet us. "Your mom and grandmother are gettin' the fire goin' in the back kitchen, rather than heat up the house."

"Did you put the horses in the barn?" I asked.

"They're all there," Ned said. "It's good that the entry to the barn is on the other side, or else your mom and grandmother would wonder what all the commotion is out there in the stable."

In the house Clara was setting the table for breakfast. "Jessie! You came home early!"

"I got homesick," I told her.

Gran appeared in the doorway to the back kitchen. "Well, look who's back. You looks like you was hauled through a knothole. I can tell you was up all night."

"We were up late, Gran, but we were quiet and didn't bother anyone. Besides, Erik came so early to pick me up, I didn't have time to fix up."

"It was right windy on the water," Erik said. "It

could've blown horns off a bull. And the sky's a bright red. We're headin' for a big storm."

"Jessie! You're home!" Mom said, coming into the kitchen.

"Dad said to pick her up early, so I did," said Erik. "Ned and I have things we want to do this mornin', and I didn't want to spend time at Gull Harbor."

"What are you goin' to do?" Gran asked.

Ned and I looked back and forth at each other. "Um, we may go out to Lonesome Isle to see if the berries are ripe," Erik said, coming to our rescue.

"Whoever knit you wasted their yarn," Gran said. "You knows right well they're not ripe yet." She stopped suddenly. "And since when do you go berryin' out there? No one goes out there."

"It's just somethin' to do, Gran," I said.

"Somethin' to do? There's plenty to do right here!"

"Leave them alone, Mother!" Mom yelled from the back kitchen. "Come and give me a hand, will you?" Mom had made bangbellies for breakfast, and since I was back, she whipped up more batter.

Once at the table I loaded the pancakes with partridgeberry jam and butter and gobbled them.

Mom shook her head. "You act like you're starvin'."

"I'm just a mite hungry." I helped myself to the last pancake on the platter.

"Go easy on the butter," Mom said. "Our little Millie Moo has been traipsin' around the fields so much she's not givin' us much milk."

Once I finished the last bite, I was so tired I could have fallen asleep on a washboard, but we had to get the rest of the horses out to the island. I got up and gave a nod toward the door. "I'm goin' to feed Blizzard and the horses."

"You look some tired, Jessie. Go on up to bed," Mom said. "The boys will feed the horses."

"Let her do it," Gran ordered. "She says she's lookin' for somethin' to do!"

"I'll do it." I had to get the rest of the ponies out onto the island. By now Melloy McCrumb and Jack Hawley must have discovered the horses were missing.

I went into the kitchen and found food from last night that Mom had saved for Blizzard. "Can I come with you to feed Raven?" Clara asked.

"Not right now," I said. "Mom needs you to help clean up."

Clara pouted, but she didn't ask again.

Back at the barn Blizzard barked and jumped on me, lapping my face. "Poor dog, we left you here all night after all you did for us," I said, putting the plate of food down for him.

The ponies looked up at me anxiously and neighed. "I'm settin' you free pretty soon," I promised them.

I took Raven's brush and stroked her neck for a moment. "You don't know what's goin' on with all these horses around, do you, my sweet girl?" She nuzzled against my shoulder and whinnied softly. I poured oats into her trough and pumped fresh water for her from the well, and then I fed the other horses. Once the ponies were on Lonesome Isle, maybe we'd put them out to pasture on the other side of the gull gaze, where no one would see them from the tickle. There was plenty of uncut grass out there.

Ned and Erik joined me in the barn. "Now what do we do?" Ned asked. "This is your show, Jessie."

"Erik, you can take the ponies one by one by boat to Lonesome Isle. Ned and I will hold each horse while you drive," I answered.

"That'll take too long," Erik said. "There are six more horses in the barn, counting Cocoa. Six trips across will take all morning."

"Besides, it's starting to blow up," Ned said uneasily. "I think we're goin' to get a storm."

"Could we take two horses at a time?" I suggested.

Ned shook his head. "No, too hard to handle in a boat."

"Then what do you suggest?" I asked.

Erik scratched his head. "I suppose we could walk them across, like you did with the others."

"The tide's in. It's too deep to walk." I had a better idea. "There's another way. I'll ride Raven and drive them all over there myself. Raven will swim—and the others will tag along. " Ned and Erik looked at each other doubtfully. "I can do it," I insisted. "The horses will follow Raven, I'm sure. She's a leader. Even Cocoa keeps out of her way and lets her eat first."

I got a horse blanket and slapped it on Raven's back. Her saddle hung nearby, and I strapped it onto her and then attached the reins. "Are you ready for this, Raven?" I whispered as I hoisted myself onto her back.

"You can't do this, Jessie," Ned said. "You don't know the other horses will even follow you."

"Blizzard's comin' with me. He helped herd the ponies last night, so they know him." I urged Raven out of the stable, and the boys followed me. "You boys get in the boat, and you can help by steering around any horse that swims off in the wrong direction."

"I've never heard of roundin' up horses with a boat," Erik said.

"Then you'll be the first," I told him. "Now bring the horses out, and we'll start by drivin' them down to the water. We've got to move fast. I don't want Mom or Clara to see us. There'd be too much explainin' and arguin'."

Erik and Ned went back to the barn, muttering to each other. They each led two ponies into the pasture and then brought out the last two. Then they removed the leads from the horses' bridles.

I clicked my heel on Raven's flank and rode around our little herd of ponies. Blizzard stood to the side, watching closely. "Come on!" I said, heading toward the beach. I was right happy when Cocoa immediately followed me. Blizzard barked and began herding. "See? We'll be fine," I called. "Bring feed from the barn when you come in the boat."

Cocoa stayed close. One of the other horses wandered off, but Blizzard chased it back into the herd.

Lonesome Isle looked far away. Taking a breath, I

clicked the reins and headed into the water with the group of ponies around me.

I drove the herd out into the tickle, noticing the motion of Raven's body change as she began to swim. A few of the other ponies hesitated as the water deepened, but at Blizzard's bark they continued to follow, their legs reaching out smoothly as they swam. Blizzard took up the rear, his legs and big paws like boat paddles.

The water was calm, but the sky was threatening. With my knees gripped tightly to Raven's sides as she swam, I sang out my own silly song in cheek music, hoping the horses would follow my voice and be unafraid.

> Lalala, little ponies, follow me, follow me,
> Into the water and out to the sea.
> Loodle-loo, loodle-loo, you're as brave as can be.
> I'll find you a safe place—lalala, looloo-lee.

Before long we reached shallow water, and Raven made her way up onto the beach. Once on dry land I called out my song, "Lalala, little ponies, follow me, follow me." The ponies came out of the water one by one, to the safety of Lonesome Isle.

CHAPTER 42

"Somethin' Mighty Strange"

The boys had been put-putting around us slowly in the boat, keeping watch. Ned sat on the bow with a long stick he would use to nudge any pony that might swim away from the herd. Now he put the rod away, and Erik steered the boat to the old island wharf. I ran over to help tie up and bring the leads back to the barn.

"Is there room enough in the barn for all the horses?" Ned asked.

"It's a huge barn," I said as we headed toward the beach and the horses.

"It'll do for now," Erik said. "Besides, it's goin' to storm." He looked up at the gulls soaring high overhead. "Gulls flying at great height, windy weather late tonight," he recited.

We hurried to the ponies, which were already grazing and rolling on the tall grass.

"Do you think anyone will suspect the horses are out here on Lonesome Isle?" Ned asked.

"They might at some point," Erik said. "But right

now folks would be more likely to think they were taken out to Stepping Stone Island, or one of the other islands closer to Gull Harbor."

After hitching the leads to the horses' bridles, we brought the horses into the barn, set them up in stalls, and wiped them down with fresh rugs the boys had brought from our barn along with the feed.

Then Erik and Ned primed the pump outside the old house with water they had brought.

"Hooray!" Erik yelled as the water gushed into pails for the horses. "There's still lots of fresh water here."

"This is one huge-sized building," Ned observed. "Your grandparents must have had lots of cattle."

"They did—cows, sheep, goats. Our grandfather delivered milk and butter to Gull Harbor," Erik said.

"And cheese," I added. "In the winter he delivered it all by dogsled."

We set up a pile of feed in each stall. "I hope we can get them out to pasture soon," I said. "I don't know how long this feed will last."

"Wouldn't the other side of the hill be better for them to graze?" Ned asked. "Then they wouldn't be seen from land."

"That's exactly what I've been thinkin', Ned," I said.

Erik frowned. "But that's where the shipwreck took place—off that side of the island."

"What Erik isn't tellin' is this," I put in. "The other side of the island is where the ghosts wail and cry."

Ned gave Erik a sideways glance. "You don't really believe that, do you?"

My brother shrugged. "I used to sneak out here to hear the hollies, but I never did hear them. Others have, though."

"It don't matter. So long as everyone thinks the island is haunted, the ponies are safe," I said.

"But neither of you heard the sounds, did you?" Ned asked again.

"Let's go," I said without answering. "We best get back before the storm hits. Come on, Blizzard. Boat!" My dog ran ahead of us to the wharf.

We shut the barn and headed down to the wharf. Ned stopped at a bush and picked off a red berry. "These red berries are blueberries, aren't they?"

"They'm red 'cause they'm green; that's why they'm not blue!" I laughed. "Get it?"

"I get it," Ned said, shoving me. "And I've heard that joke before, Jessie."

"If Gran figures out we've gone to Lonesome Isle,

we can truly tell her we came to check for blueberries,"
Erik said.

"There won't be any blueberries once the ponies
get at them," I pointed out.

When we got into the boat with Blizzard and
headed home, Ned pointed to the whitecaps. "White
horses! Another sign of bad weather." I could see that
Ned wasn't completely over his fear of storms since
the shipwreck.

Dad's boat was back when we arrived at our cove.
"Don't tell *anyone*—including Dad—what we've done,"
I whispered.

"He'll find out sooner or later, Jessie," Erik said.

"Let it be later," I replied.

I washed up in the back kitchen, where the fire was
going in the wood stove. I could smell baked beans
simmering. When I went to my room and took off my
dirty clothes, the stink of horses out-smelled everything.
Whew! I changed quickly and then stuffed my clothes
in a bag, which I hid way back in my bedroom closet.

We must have looked tired because when I came
downstairs, Mom made us an early supper of baked
beans, ham, and potatoes.

"What did you do out on the island?" Dad asked me.

"We just . . . uh . . . ," I stammered.

Ned came to my rescue. "We checked for blueberries. They aren't ripe."

Gran sniffed. "You don't say."

"Well, there's lots of excitement in Gull Harbor, let me tell," Dad said. "You'd never believe what took place down there."

"What happened, Dad?" I asked.

"Seems like someone stole all of Melloy McCrumb's ponies durin' the night."

"Go away with ya!" Erik did a great job of looking astonished.

"Must've been a group of men," Dad said. "No way one person could handle all those ponies."

Gran chuckled. "Melloy McCrumb and Jack Hawley must be as cross as cats."

"They're both fightin' mad, let me tell." Dad tried to stifle a snigger, but then burst out laughing. "I wish I could have seen Melloy's face when he discovered the horses were missin'."

"Someone sure put it over on him, didn't they?" Mom was giggling too.

Dad went on, still chuckling. "Everyone in town is having a hoot on McCrumb."

Gran shook her head. "I sure wouldn't want to be the one who stole the horses. That tough barnacle Melloy McCrumb will be out for blood."

I scooped more beans onto my plate. "So, did you get a lot of fish, Dad?"

"Aye, we did, and dropped them all off down the harbor at the plant. But we brought home a few for Clara to gut." Dad playfully tugged at Clara's hair.

I was quiet during the rest of the supper. When we were finished, I yawned. "Erik picked me up so early this mornin' that I'm cowed out. If you don't mind, Mom, I'd like to go to bed."

"You must be tired, Jessie," Mom replied. "Go on to bed. Gran and I will take care of cleanin' up tonight."

As I undressed, I began to worry. What if Melloy McCrumb showed up here looking for the ponies? Dad could honestly say he knew nothing about it. But part of me wanted to tell him. If Dad knew, he'd be more likely to protect us. But I was too tired to think about anything. I'd tell him in the morning.

As soon as my head hit the pillow, I fell asleep,

still seeing the ponies and hearing their hoofbeats all scrambled up in my dreams.

I slept right through the night into the next morning and finally woke at the sound of loud voices down in the house. Clara was crying, and Mom was trying to console her.

I climbed out of bed and tiptoed to the stairway. What was wrong? I looked out from the hall window and could see Dad's boat was gone. Oh, no! Now I couldn't tell him all that happened, and he wouldn't be here to help us. I was afraid to hear what was going on as I entered the kitchen.

"Cocoa has gone away," Clara sobbed when she saw me. "I went out to the barn and . . . he wasn't there." She sniffed. "Raven's gone too."

"Clara, they're not missing," I said. "They're just over on the island—oh!" I slapped my hand over my mouth, but it was too late.

"See?" Mom said softly to Clara, who was sitting on her lap. "Cocoa is fine." She looked up at me. "What are they doing over there?"

"I—uh, I rode Raven over there—to check out the berries. Cocoa followed me."

Gran planted her hands on her hips. "I thought you kids went over there by boat."

"Erik and Ned went by boat, but I went on Raven." I looked around the kitchen. "So Dad went fishing? I thought there might be a storm today."

"He and Uncle George left before dawn," Mom answered. "The sunrise was bright red. I have to admit I'm a little worried."

"Don't scrimshank, Jessie." Gran eyed me suspiciously. "Somethin's goin' on you're not tellin' us. You were up most of the night at your slumber party and came back early in the mornin'. At dawn, as I understands it."

I nodded. "Yes, Gran. I came home at dawn yesterday when Erik came for me. I'm done in. And I'd probably still be asleep, 'cept I heard Clara crying." I turned and headed for the stairs. "I'm goin' back to bed."

Gran blocked my way to the stairway. "You were right tired yesterday. Yet, instead of goin' to bed, you rides Raven out to Lonesome Isle? This seems mighty strange to me. Don't tell me you went out there for berries—or for *somethin' to do*." Gran put her hands on my shoulders and forced me to look her in the eyes. "Jessie, I knows you've been up to somethin'. And I think you'd better tell us all about it *right now*."

CHAPTER 43

Melloy McCrumb Has Landed!

"Come on, Jessie. Out with it!" Gran urged. "What have you done?"

Gran's dark eyes seemed to cut right through me. I'd have to tell them the truth, but would they understand how much the ponies meant to us girls?

I turned toward my mother. "Oh, Mom, please don't be mad," I began, hoping she would be more understanding than my grandmother.

"Don't be mad at Jessie!" Clara wailed. "Don't punish her."

"Hush, my child," Mom whispered. "We would never hurt Jessie."

I stammered, trying to get the words out. "Me and my friend-girls . . . we took Melloy McCrumb's ponies from Gull Harbor and put 'em out on Lonesome Isle."

Mom blinked her eyes as if waking from a dream. "You . . . you *what*? You girls stole that entire herd of horses?"

"No, Mom, we didn't steal them. We *rescued* them."

"Good morrow to you!" Gran sputtered. "You're tellin' us that you brought each and every one of those horses all the way up here from Gull Harbor?"

"And then all the way out to the island?" Mom added. "Who helped you?"

"Meta and the Doyle twins . . ."

"Aha!" Gran broke in. "That's what you did on your so-called slumber party. You had it all planned to take those ponies away that night."

"We *had* to do it. The meat wagon was comin' the next mornin' to take those poor little horses off to be killed."

"You girls couldn't have done this all by yourselves. Someone else is involved," Mom said.

"Well, Erik and Ned helped, but only after we got the horses out here."

"Oh," Mom moaned, "I can only imagine what Melloy will do once he finds out."

"Who's goin' to tell him?" I asked. "The girls swore they'd never tell."

"Secrets are never kept for long," Mom said.

"By the same token you took Clara right out from

under Melloy's nose, and he already has it in for us," Gran warned.

"Aye, he's sure to come out here in a rage," Mom agreed. "And Dad's gone out on the water for a couple of days, so we're on our own if those men show up." Mom slipped Clara from her lap. "If Melloy finds Clara out here too, he's sure to want her back."

"No!" Clara yowled. "Don't let him get me."

"Hush, Clara!" Gran ordered. "Remember, we have papers from Uncle Don and your uncle Joseph giving you to us."

"Hmm, I wonder if Melloy can read when we show him the documents," Mom said thoughtfully.

"He can't read; I'll go bail for it. And even if he could, it's all in legal mumbo jumbo," Gran added. "We need a Mountie to enforce our right to Clara, or Melloy will never believe it."

Clara began whimpering, and Mom gave her a kiss. "Oh, don't worry about the McCrumbs today. There's a storm brewing, and they won't be showin' up here—not yet, anyway. Everything will be all right, my child, once Dad is back."

Gran turned to me. "Jessie, you watch Clara for a while! Your mother and I need to talk." She and Mom headed to the back kitchen, and I could hear Gran grumbling. "Imagine those girls takin' the horses!"

I couldn't hear Mom's answer.

"Want to go play ducks and drakes?" Clara asked, tugging at my arm. I let her lead me outside. "I'm gettin' better at skippin' stones, Jessie."

We headed down to the wharf with Blizzard trotting happily alongside us. The sky was filled with ominous clouds, and the water was dark but motionless, like the calm before a gale. *Maybe Dad will come back before it storms*, I hoped. *Everything would be all right if Dad were only here.*

Clara busied herself collecting smooth thin stones to play our game, then stood on the shoreline with me. I took the first stone and threw it level across the surface, where it began to skip.

"A *duck* and a *drake* and a *double pancake*, and a *penny* to pay the old baker . . . ," we sang.

"Ooops, that's only four skips," I said. "I didn't make it to the end of the song."

"Help me skip a stone."

I picked out a flat stone and placed it in Clara's palm. "Hold your hand like this. Now we'll do it together." We sliced the stone into the air over the top of the water. It skipped, making little circles that rippled out into larger ones and then faded. "*A hop hop scotch* in another old *notch* . . . Oh, Clara. Look! You did three this time!"

Blizzard barked and jumped into the water. We both laughed as he dove to fetch the stone. Finally, he swam back with another rock in his mouth, which he deposited at our feet. Blizzard shook himself, casting water everywhere.

Suddenly we heard the sound of an engine. A boat was pulling into our little harbor. One man was at the wheel, and another man stood next to him. Blizzard began to bark frantically.

"Oh, no! It's the McCrumbs' boat!" I cried. "Run, Clara!"

Clara screamed, flew up the stairs, then raced to the house with Blizzard and me following after.

CHAPTER 44

Storm Brewin'

Clara, Blizzard, and I raced into the kitchen, the door slamming behind us.

"Mom!" I yelled. "Melloy McCrumb's boat is in the barrasway. Jack Hawley's with him."

"He saw me—I know he saw me!" Clara ran to my mother, who pulled her into her arms.

"What'll we do? They're hitchin' up their boat right now!" I yelped.

At that moment Ned and Erik flew into the house. "We saw McCrumb's boat from the hill," Erik told us breathlessly.

Gran came in from the back kitchen. "I just saw Melloy and Jack headin' this way, and they're both carryin' rifles!"

"Rifles!" We all shrieked at once.

Erik darted to the kitchen door and bolted it, while Ned did the same to the back kitchen entry. We hardly ever used the front door, so it was always kept locked these days.

"I'll take Clara upstairs and get her out of sight." Mom grabbed Clara's hand and pulled her to the stairway just as pounding began on the kitchen door. Blizzard started barking and pawing the door.

"Go away or we'll sic our dog on you!" Erik yelled.

"No!" I whispered. "They'd shoot him." I patted my dog. "Be quiet, boy."

Mom came into the kitchen. "Clara's shut in my room with your old dolls, Jessie. She promised to be quiet and not cry."

"Open up!" Melloy McCrumb yelled as he banged the door with his foot. "We're right sure you took our horses."

"We don't have any horses here!" Erik shouted. "Go look in the barn and you'll see for yourself."

"It looks like horse tracks out by your barn, and they weren't made by one horse!" Jack Hawley bellowed. "We want those horses back."

"We ain't leavin' until you give up those horses!" McCrumb sounded determined. "And by the way, I saw my daughter down by the wharf. We ain't movin' till you bring her out too."

"Make yourselves comfortable, boys, 'cause we're not openin' the door for you," Mom called out.

"'By the way'!" Gran sputtered. "Clara's just an afterthought as far as he's concerned."

"Second only to the horses," I added.

Gran stomped off into the back kitchen.

Erik turned to Mom and me. "I don't like those two hotheaded fools with loaded guns parked at our door." He spoke softly.

"We need a Mountie here," Ned whispered.

Erik nodded. "I'm thinkin' I should go get Chet Young from the Harbor."

"You can't leave," I protested in a low voice. "We need you and Ned here to protect our family."

Gran came out of the back kitchen with two rifles. She reached into her apron pocket and pulled out some long brass bullets, which she stuffed into them *Where did she learn to load guns?* I wondered

"They've got rifles, and so do we," she said, shoving a gun at each of the boys. "The safety is on, but be careful just the same. We don't want any accidents."

"I want my horses and my daughter right now!" Melloy barked.

"It's not enough that your girl Jessie ruined my son; you stole our horses, too," Jack Hawley added.

"You might as well go on home!" Gran hollered. "You're not gettin' into this house."

"We ain't leavin', old woman!" Melloy McCrumb replied. "Even if we have to break down the door."

"Aw, Melloy . . ." Jack spoke in a low tone, but we all could hear him. "Shoot the gun in the air. That ought to scare 'em into opening the door."

"Don't you try anything with guns!" Gran yelled. "I've got a gun too, and believe you me, I know how to shoot."

"Ha!" McCrumb and Hawley both burst out laughing. "The old lady thinks she's a sharpshooter."

"I don't like all this talk about guns," I said. "You boys must stay, but I'm goin' to get the Mountie. Is there gas in our old boat?"

"I filled the tank this mornin'," Erik whispered.

"Jessie, there's a storm brewin'. It's starting to rain," Mom pleaded. "Stay here with us."

"I'm goin' to get help," I answered. "Storm or no storm."

"I'm ascared for you, maid. The waves in a storm can be mountainous," Gran said.

"We need help from the Mountie, and I'm goin' now."

"It will take an hour to get there, and an hour back," Ned said. "What'll we do with these crazy men in the meantime?"

"Just keep them outside somehow." I was already heading for my oilskin coat and linkum hat.

"These men are out for blood. They'll likely go after you in their boat, Jessie," Mom warned.

"Not if I tow their boat away."

"That'll make 'em all the more vicious," Ned whispered.

"I'll take care of them if they gets vicious," Gran said, taking the rifle from Erik.

"Do whatever you have to do, but give me time to get away."

I had to sneak off to the wharf now, but that might be right hard with Melloy McCrumb and Jack Hawley camped out at our door!

CHAPTER 45

Dangerous Seas

Mom shook her head. "Oh, Jessie, I have a bad feelin' about this storm. It's hard enough to make it through the tickle all by yourself. But once you're out on the open water with those breakers . . ."

"I've caused all this trouble, and I'm goin' to take care of it."

"Now, Jessie." Gran still carried the rifle under her arm. "You sure have sown a wind and reaped a whirl-wind with all that you've done. But you can't make it better if you're swept overboard in a storm."

"There are life jackets on board," I said as I pulled on the oilskin coat and hat. "I'm leavin' the back way before McCrumb and Hawley think of that door. But you and Ned need to keep 'em talkin', so I can get away."

"Oh, Jessie, my child, you must stay right here," Mom insisted.

"I will be all right, I promise, and if the goin' is rough, I'll head to shore."

"I have confidence in Jessie," Erik said. "She does know her way through the tickle. She proved it to me the other night."

"But there were two of you," Mom said.

The banging on the door was loud now, and Melloy yelled, "Open up! We want those horses. Tell us where they are."

"We have no idea!" Erik hollered.

I went to the back kitchen, with Gran, Mom, and the boys following me. "Go to the door and keep those barnacles talkin' so I can get away."

To my surprise, Gran put her arms around me, then kissed me on the cheek. "Be careful, my child."

"Jessie . . ." Mom began to cry. "I wish you'd stay."

"I'll be fine." I opened the back door quietly. Blizzard's tail wagged furiously, and he pushed his way out, but I pulled him back. "No, Blizzard," I whispered. My dog's tail drooped, and he looked at me with sad eyes.

It was pouring as I ran from the back of the house to the wharf. Since I heard no outcries, I assumed Melloy McCrumb and Jack Hawley hadn't seen me.

I climbed into the old boat, removed the cover, and started up the engine, hoping no one could hear it over the pelting rain. Before I untied the boat and backed out, I went to the McCrumbs' boat, undid the lines, and then tied their bowline to the stern of my boat.

After maneuvering the two boats away from the wharf, I headed out into the darkening waters of Stony Tickle, with the McCrumbs' boat bobbing behind me.

Once I was around the bend and a few hundred feet from our little bay, I untied Melloy's boat and watched as it drifted farther and farther away. "That'll keep them from following me," I muttered.

The tickle was beginning to get rough as the wind blew hard. Usually the tickle was calm, being protected by the mainland on one side and the island on the other. As I made my way through the darkening water, I realized once again how difficult it was to drive the boat and look for the sunkers at the same time—let alone in the driving rain.

Could I make it to Gull Harbor? I wondered. Once I got through the tickle and out into the open water, what would the sea be like? This wasn't just rain; it was a bad storm with high winds. If only Dad were here!

As I slipped through the tickle, with the wind blowing toward me, I thought I heard wails coming from Lonesome Isle. I shuddered as I remembered the stories of storms and the sea creatures that lured ships to the rocks and reefs. What good would it all be if this boat sank with me in it?

"Dear Lord," I prayed, aloud, "I'm sorry for causing so much trouble. I only wanted to save Clara and the ponies. Please stay with me and help me to get to Gull Harbor."

I cut the engine to slow and tried to see ahead where I thought the giant's head would be. Then I realized that the waves were different—circling on spots ahead of me. *Skerries!* I'd forgotten about the skerries, where underwater shoals and rocks break in rough seas.

There it is—the giant's head. If I watch carefully, the skerries will show me where the other sunkers are. I blinked my eyes and watched for the motion of the water.

It seemed like ages as I put-putted through the dangerous tickle. But now I had come to the open water, where the waves were huge. The boat rose and plunged as I drove through them. One moment I'd be looking *down* at the water, and the next I'd be looking *up* at the great swells ahead of me. It was hard to hold the boat on course. My hands were stiff and aching from gripping the wheel.

I had to keep the bow pointed into the waves, or the boat would turn and take on water broadside. I wished I had put on a life jacket, but it was too late now. I couldn't let go or I'd swamp. *I mustn't let go. I mustn't let go*, I kept telling myself.

Then my heart seemed to stop. A huge breaker was heading toward me—so high it actually blotted out the sky. I held on to the wheel and closed my eyes as I felt the boat rise. *Please stay with me, Lord*, I prayed. As the boat rose out of the water onto the breaking wave, the propeller roared, spinning in the air. Then, SMACK! The boat slapped down again. Water from the wave poured into the boat and over me.

The water in the boat was over my ankles. If another big wave broke over me, I knew I'd sink!

CHAPTER 46

A Welcome Sight

Suddenly a flash of lightning lit up the sky, and straight away there was a crack of thunder! I had to get to shore, but I couldn't risk going up on the rocks along the unfamiliar shoreline here.

Another bolt of lightning, like a chain, dropped from the clouds to the sea. The instant roar of thunder that blasted from the sky was a sure sign that the storm was right on top of me.

A light blinked on a cliff. Gull Harbor! *Hold on, Jessie!* I squinted against the rain and made out the entrance into the harbor. "Thank you, God," I whispered as I steered the boat into the calmer waters of the bay.

As I pulled up to the community wharf, relief surged over me. Dad's new boat was tied up at the dock. He had come into the harbor to get away from the storm. Everything would be fine now. Dad would know exactly what to do.

I figured Dad had probably spent the night at the

Rideouts', so after tying the boat up I raced up the steps to the main road. I was about to head to Meta's house when I saw the lights on at the bakery and ran over there instead. I peeked in through the panes of the rain-swept window, and there was my father, having coffee with Uncle George Rideout—and Chet Young!

I rushed into the bakery and directly to the table where Dad was seated. His mouth dropped open when he saw me. "Oh, my blessed Lord! Jessie! How did you get here?" His eyes scanned my soaking hair and face, then shifted to the floor, where the rain was dripping off my slicker, making puddles under my feet.

"I came in the old boat," I said.

"In this storm?" He threw his arms around me, then held me away, looking into my eyes with fear. "Why? Is something wrong at the Cliffs?"

"Melloy McCrumb and Jack Hawley are out there with rifles."

"Rifles?" Chet Young jumped from his chair. "Now what are those crazy men up to?"

"They must be after somethin'," Uncle George said, getting to his feet.

"They want Clara. They must know she's there," Dad said.

"Dad, it's not just Clara they want."

"What, then?" My father looked bewildered.

"The ponies."

"The . . . ponies? Raven and Cocoa?" Dad asked.

"No, all the ponies. All twelve of them," I explained.

Dad, Chet, and Uncle George were too stunned to speak. Chet's mouth moved . . . but without words. Then he said, "Do you mean the horses that were taken from the corral here in town?"

I nodded. "When I was stayin' over the Doyles' house, the girls and I took the ponies to save them. We herded them down the fairy path to the Cliffs. Then we brought them over to Lonesome Isle." I looked at the three men's astonished faces. "Melloy McCrumb and Jack Hawley don't know where they are. They just figured we took them."

Dad frowned as if trying to figure it all out. "You're tellin' me that you stole the ponies."

"Dad, we didn't *steal* them." I stomped my foot. "We saved their lives!"

Dad looked stunned for a few moments. Then he held up two yellow envelopes that were on the table and handed them to me. "That explains these telegrams. They're to you, Jessie. I was a little worried when they arrived, so I opened them. One is from your cousin Sandra. The other is from someone we don't know." Dad turned to the other men. "I couldn't figure 'em out, but now that Jessie's confessed about stealing the ponies . . ."

"We did *not* steal them," I stressed again.

I was about to open the telegrams when Chet said, "Don't stop to read them now, Jessie. We've got to get a move on. I don't like the idea of Melloy and Jack goin' out to your place with guns. You never know what they might do if they're mad enough."

Dad grabbed his jacket. "Let's go the once."

"Come on, Walt, and you too, George. We'll take the patrol boat." Chet opened the door, and we all rushed to the dock.

"I'll follow in the new boat," Dad said. "We'll get the old boat later."

"Jessie, why didn't Mom show Melloy the document from Uncle Don?" Dad asked as he started the boat. "After all, it's an order from the minister of justice."

"He was too cross. We were afraid to ever open

the door to him with that gun on us. Let's go, please, please."

Chet pushed us out. "So you girls . . . er . . . saved the ponies." He shook his head. "Hard to believe."

Dad put his arm around my shoulder. "Not that hard to believe—if you know my Jessie."

CHAPTER 47

Gun Talk

Even in our new boat the ride back to the Cliffs was rough. But it didn't take as long, with the government boat ahead of us blazing the way. When we arrived at our wharf, the men jumped out and secured the boats. "Wait here, Jessie," Dad ordered, "until we find out what's goin' on."

I stayed on the bottom step, straining my ears for any sounds, but I heard nothing—not even Blizzard's bark, which usually signaled a boat's approach. What was happening? I crept up the steps and peered through the rain. Suddenly I felt a poke in my back— the muzzle of a rifle!

"I've got you now, you pelt of a tripe!" Melloy McCrumb had come out from the bushes and was prodding me with his gun. "You're the one who's caused all this trouble. Now, you tell me where my horses are!"

I was so ascared I could hardly speak. "You b-b-better put that rifle down! Our Mountie's here now."

"Quit talkin' and get walkin'." He nudged me ahead of him. "Your folks will give up once they see I have you."

Could Jack Hawley have captured my dad and the others? I finally found the courage to ask. "Where's Jack Hawley?"

"Where do you suppose he is, after your grandma shot the hat right off his head! All he was doin' was shootin' at a tree to give 'em a scare, when she opened the window and took a potshot at him. He hightailed it out of here and headed back to the Harbor on the trail."

"My gran shot a gun?"

"As if you didn't know! She thinks she's Annie Oakley. But she won't start shootin' now that I've got *you*."

When we came to the house, McCrumb shoved me with the rifle. "Tell 'em I've got you and they'd better get out here quick."

"Dad!" I yelled. "I'm outside with Melloy McCrumb. He has his gun on me."

"And an itchy trigger finger!" McCrumb bellowed.

Chet opened the door. "Melloy, don't make matters worse. Let Jessie go right now."

"I want my horses!" he demanded.

"Oh, we thought you'd come for Clara."

McCrumb hesitated. "Oh, Clara . . . well, yeah. I want her, too."

"Let's clear something up. Clara isn't your ward anymore," Chet replied, papers in one hand and his pistol in the other. "These documents give the Whellers custody of Clara from now on."

Melloy McCrumb eyed Chet's pistol and lowered his rifle. I scooted over to Chet's side.

"I'm Clara's guardian," Melloy argued.

"Not anymore. You won't be getting a monthly check, either," Dad said.

"All the more reason I need the horses. They were worth money to me. I wants 'em back."

"Oh, give it up, Melloy. You don't have any claim to those ponies," Chet said.

Dad came out the door, with Ned and Erik following closely behind. "Jessie has some telegrams you should hear, Melloy. Read your telegrams, Jessie. I'm sure Melloy won't want to turn the ponies into horse meat once he hears what those telegrams have to say."

I'd almost forgotten about the telegrams! What was Dad talking about?

CHAPTER 48

Famous Ponies

The first telegram was from Sandra. I stood in the lighted entryway and read it out loud.

```
Shared your letter with everyone
STOP Friends at our stable want two
ponies STOP I want Moonstruck STOP
Radio TV stations will contact you
STOP SANDRA
```

"This is some shockin' good news!" I exclaimed. "Three ponies already have homes!"

"What's this all about?" Melloy grunted. "How does these people down in Boston know about my ponies?" He frowned, and then, as if a light were going on in his head, he exclaimed, "Aha! You and your friends *did* steal my horses!"

"No, Jessie and her friend-girls rescued a dozen doomed horses that didn't belong to anyone," Dad said brusquely. "Now go on, Jessie; read the next telegram."

I unfolded the next envelope. "It's from the radio station in Boston," I said, and began to read:

```
Your letter regarding the plight
of the Newfoundland Ponies was
read on our Boston Morning program
STOP Our listeners are calling and
sending donations for your shelter
STOP Our program was picked up by
other radio and television stations
throughout the US and Canada STOP
Animal lovers from both countries
have started campaigns to raise
money to save ponies STOP

Our TV photographers and reporter
will be coming to Gull Harbor
STOP Canadian affiliates are
also sending their staff STOP Bob
Raymond from Boston Morning
```

"Don't you see?" Dad said when I finished. "Your letter to Sandra was read on the radio, and now radio and TV stations in Canada and the States are jumpin' on the bandwagon to save these *famous* ponies."

"This was all your idea, Jessie!" Ned exclaimed. "You'll probably be famous too."

Melloy McCrumb spoke up. "Famous! If anyone should be famous, it's me! I'm the one who corralled them horses from the islands. I'm the one that saved them from dyin' out there."

We all laughed. "You were goin' to make them into horse meat!" Chet said. "And I'm sure that will be told on the radio and television too."

At Chet's words Melloy McCrumb grabbed his rifle and headed toward the woods. "I'm goin' to walk back to Gull Harbor—since *someone* stole my boat. Don't let that daft grandmother hold a gun on me!" he yelled over his shoulder. "She aimed for Jack and almost hit him."

"If my mother wanted to hit him, she would have," Dad said. "She can shoot the wings off a mosquito."

"When I find out who stole my boat," he muttered, "I'll tell *that* on television; you can go bail for it!"

Chet put his pistol in its holster. "Go wait in my boat, Melloy. I'll give you a ride back to the Harbor, and we can look for your boat along the way."

Melloy muttered as he headed down to the wharf.

"Well, the rain's let up. The wind's changed. I'll be leavin'." Chet shook hands with all of us. "I hope Melloy's boat ain't up on the rocks somewhere.

Maybe he and Jack will go back to fishing instead of their harebrained schemes to make money." He buttoned up his jacket. "Odd how that boat just . . . disappeared."

"I might have helped it—er . . . just a little . . . somehow," I said.

"Uh-huh," Chet said with a twinkle in his eye. "I'm sure that's just what happened. *Somehow!*"

CHAPTER 49

Television Documentary

The week that Mr. Raymond and his staff from Boston arrived in Gull Harbor was the most exciting time anyone had ever seen. A Canadian news service joined in, and both groups went out to Lonesome Isle on several flat-bottomed barges. They brought cameras and trucks and other supplies and camped out to photograph our pretty herd of ponies.

I couldn't help but wonder, had the crews heard the hollies? Did they know the story of the shipwreck and how the ghosts walked the island? I just had to find out.

One morning I took the little boat and went out to Lonesome Isle by myself. The radio teams had built a new dock closer to the horses, and I coasted in smoothly. Mr. Raymond, whom I'd met earlier, came out to greet me and show me around.

After we browsed around the cameras and trucks and he explained some of the equipment, we sat down on folding chairs and had coffee, which someone had made over a gas grill.

"So, Mr. Raymond, you all slept outside or in the trucks for the past few days?" I asked.

"Not too comfortable, but we've done this many a time," he answered. "It's been cold and windy since we arrived."

"We get lots of windy days in August—sometimes gales. Did everyone sleep well . . . with the sounds of the wind and sea?"

Mr. Raymond interrupted with a grin. "You're asking if we heard the ghosts, aren't you?"

I dug the toe of my shoe in the sand and felt my face redden. "I . . . I guess you've heard the stories, then."

"Oh, we'll be talking about that on the radio and in the TV documentary we're doing," he said. "People are always interested in ghost stories." He sipped on his coffee.

"So, did you hear the hollies—the wails of the ghosts?"

"Oh, sure we heard them!" He chuckled. "They were real noisy one night." I must have looked comical struck, because he laughed again. "I suspect you heard them too, Jessie."

"I sure did."

"Do you believe in ghosts?"

"It's a lot of pishogue." I hesitated, then added, "But I really did hear them."

"You're not the only one, Jessie. Those wails were enough to scare the entire crew. So the next morning we decided we'd find out what made those awful screams. Want to see what we found?"

"I . . . I guess so." Mr. Raymond took my hand and pulled me up from the chair. Then we headed up the path to the gull gaze. This time we turned onto another path that I hadn't seen before. After a few minutes it came to an abrupt end at the foot of a cliff.

"Look up there." Mr. Raymond pointed to a gaping hole in the cliff. "It's a cave. Some of my boys climbed up there and went inside. Want to climb up?"

"No, it's too steep," I said. "What's in there?"

"Nothing, but there's another small hole inside that opens to the other side of the island. We figured out that when the wind is blowing hard from the ocean side, it blows through, and that small hole acts like a whistle. A big loud whistle! That's what everyone's been hearing."

"No, go on with you. A whistle?"

"A natural whistle. If you go up to the cave, you'll hear the sound of the sea on the other side. But when it's real windy—well, that's when the wailing starts."

"So there are no hollies? No ghosts?"

"Naw! It's a lot of . . . what do you call it? *Pishogue!*"

We went down to the grassy meadow where the horses grazed and played. The television crews from Canada had arrived, and the place was busy with people and trucks and cameras. Since there was no electricity, the crews started up loud, whirring generators, which turned on bright lights.

The ponies stopped whatever they were doing, looked up, then ran away. But eventually their curiosity got the best of them. Cautiously some of them came closer and closer until one of our brave little horses actually went right up to a cameraman and peered into the camera lens.

Raven was out on the island with the others so she could be in the movie too. When she saw me, she trotted over and nudged me. "You want me to ride?" I asked her. I climbed on her back, and we took off through the pasture and then across a long, sandy stretch of beach. I wondered if Raven felt like we were part of the wind, as I did with my long hair flowing out behind me like Raven's long mane.

The cameramen loved this scene and followed us around in a pickup truck as we galloped over the rocks and sand and then splashed into the water, stirring up wavelets sparkling in the sun.

Raven must have known she was being filmed. She did everything right—even adding a touch of humor to the show when she bit a cameraman's cap and tossed it from his head into the berry bushes.

"That horse plays right to the camera," Mr. Raymond said, laughing.

The next day my friends and I were invited to Lonesome Isle to watch the filming. The girls dressed up in their church clothes to be interviewed. I still wore my jeans, but that was okay, Mr. Raymond told me. He asked us girls all sorts of questions. "Were you scared to do this daring hike into the dark woods to hide the ponies?"

"I was right scared," Margie piped up. "I even fell into the brook! I was freezing and I wanted to go home. But I stayed on."

"Howsomever, she sure cried a lot!" Brianna interrupted.

"In the long run you girls worked together as a team to get these horses to safety." Mr. Raymond turned to the people who had come to watch—practically the entire town of Gull Harbor. "Let's give these six heroines of Lonesome Isle a cheer!" There were whistles and applause and yelling, and I don't think I'd ever felt so happy and embarrassed in all my born days.

Then Erik and Ned were interviewed. They explained how stunned they were when they discovered us and then told their part in the rescue.

Ned mentioned the shipwreck at Devil's Head. "The Whellers saved our lives," he said. "They took us in, and we became friends."

"The Whellers took me in too," Clara added—surprisingly, as she seemed shy around the cameras.

Mr. Raymond turned the microphone to Gran, who stood by with Clara. "You have an amazing and hospitable family, Mrs. Wheller."

"Well, it turned out that we were just being kind to angels," Gran said, "because *we* were the ones who were blessed. Like the old Scripture tells us, 'Do not forget hospitality, for through it some, unknown to themselves, entertained angels.'"

CHAPTER 50

Party Time

Red, yellow, and white balloons danced into the sky a few days later as the Canadian TV crew filmed scenes on Lonesome Isle. A band from White Falls played Newfoundland folk music while couples and children danced. Families picnicked on the grass. Even Melloy McCrumb and his wife showed up. I spotted Mike Hawley mixing with the kids too. He still wore a cast on one arm, and he limped as he walked.

Mr. Bluet, the famous Canadian television host, sauntered among the crowd with a cameraman and a microphone and came to stop by Melloy McCrumb. "What part did you have in this adventure, Mr. McCrumb?" he asked.

"I was the one who took those abandoned horses off the islands," Melloy McCrumb boasted. "Didn't want to see anything bad happen to those poor beasts."

But it was too late for Melloy McCrumb to take any credit for saving the horses. Mr. Bluet quickly recognized him as the infamous man who would sell the horses for horse meat.

Mr. Bluet interviewed many of the Gull Harbor folks on camera, including kids who were not part of our adventure. Everyone had gathered in the pasture and was sitting on the grass.

"So, how do you kids feel about the ponies?" Mr. Bluet asked. A member of the crew passed a mike into the crowd.

One by one kids from Gull Harbor answered. "We're so proud of Jessie."

"I'm glad Jessie saved the ponies."

I took the microphone from Mr. Bluet. "Thank you, but it wasn't just me, remember. It took six of us to take the horses away that night. Then my brother Erik and his friend Ned helped get the ponies out here to Lonesome Isle."

"We would have helped you too, Jessie," one boy said.

"We'd have been right happy to help," several kids added.

Mr. Bluet leaned over and spoke into the mike. "It looks like there are kids and families who want to help you with the ponies. What needs to be done, Jessie?"

"We'll need the stalls cleaned and the horses

groomed," I replied. "Maybe families could come and cut hay. We'll need enough to last all winter."

"We'll do it, Jessie!"

"Don't forget, these things need to be done regular-like. Can't get noody-nawdy and lackadaisical a month from now," I reminded them.

"We won't get noody-nawdy!" several kids yelled.

"We'll help as long as the ponies need us, won't we?" called out another voice.

"Yes, just tell us what to do."

Mr. Bluet spoke into the mike. "Jessie, why don't you sign up everyone who wants to help out." He handed me his yellow writing pad. "Kids, if you sign this, you've made a contract. You don't back out later. Right?"

"Right!" The kids cheered and clapped.

Suddenly a silence fell over the crowd as Mike Hawley limped up to me. "Will you count me in, Jessie?" he asked.

I was so comical struck I couldn't speak. After all the trouble he'd caused, now he wanted to join us?

The kids were quiet, waiting to hear how I'd answer, and here I was at a loss for words.

"Wasn't your father working with Mr. McCrumb to sell the ponies?" Mr. Bluet asked Mike.

"I didn't know what Dad was goin' to do with the horses," Mike said. "In fact one of those ponies— Star—was mine. When I heard Pa brought him back from Stepping Stone, I was some happy. But then he said we couldn't keep him anymore and Star was goin' to another home. And then I was sad. I didn't know my pony was goin' to be . . . killed." For a minute I thought Mike was going to cry, but he held back the tears. He pointed to his cast with his free hand. "I can't do much, but I really wants to help somehow."

Mike looked so pathetic and so miserable I forgot to be angry. I wrote down his name on the yellow pad. "You're first on the list, Mike," I said.

We felt gloomy when the radio and television people left to go back to Boston and Ottawa. Before Mr. Bluet, Mr. Raymond, and the others left, they told us to get busy and find a place where we could watch ourselves on television. The program would be on in the fall. Maybe we'd have television sets ourselves by then, we hoped.

"What will the name of the program be?" I asked.

"*Kids Save Doomed Ponies,*" Mr. Bluet answered.

CHAPTER 51

Angels

The following summer, during the months of June and July, I finally went to visit Sandra in Boston. She took me to a nearby stable where Moonstruck and the other two Newfoundland ponies were boarded.

"Do you think she remembers me?" I asked as I stroked Moonstruck's soft nose.

"Of course she does," Sandra replied.

After a wonderful two months of touring Boston, shopping, riding trails with Sandra through the reservation, and even speaking on *Boston Morning*, it was time to return to Newfoundland.

By now I was eager to go back to the stony crags of home. It was summer again, and I missed the blue-gray cliffs and the clownish puffins that snuggled their nests into their walls; I missed the eagles and fish hawks that soared overhead.

Dad, Erik, and Ned, who was back visiting us again, met me at Gull Harbor in the new boat. Blizzard leaped and jumped around like a giant puppy when he first saw me get off the steamer. "I missed you too," I told him as he lapped my face.

Ned grinned. "This place is dull when you're not around."

"Causin' trouble," Erik finished.

"You've cut your hair!" Dad said, looking disappointed. "Where's you braid?"

"I had it cut off in Boston at Sandra's hairdresser," I replied.

"It makes you look older," Ned said. "But it's nice," he added quickly.

I sat up near the bow with Blizzard next to me, his head and front legs spread across my lap.

As our boat came through Stony Tickle, the water capped with white foam and breaking around the old sunkers that had been there since the world began, I saw the giant's hand through the ripples. "He's waving to me," I called out to Dad and the boys.

Mom, Clara, and Gran must have heard the engine, because they were on the dock waiting for us as we glided into our little harbor.

After hugs and kisses from Mom and Clara—and a peck on the cheek from Gran—I ran to the beach to look out at Lonesome Isle with Clara by my side.

"Let's go out there. I want to see the horses."

"Some folks have sent their ponies to us for protection," Mom said. "So we have a larger herd right now."

Clara nodded. "We have twelve ponies again."

"And a few more on the way," Mom added.

"But come eat first," Gran called. "We want to hear all about your trip."

"I've made a big Jiggs dinner," Mom said. "All in your honor."

"I'm starving," I said, "but first I want to see Raven. Is she all right? Has she . . ."

"Raven's been free roaming out on Lonesome Isle ever since you've been gone, Jessie." Dad said with a wink at Mom. "I think Jessie should go out and see Raven before dinner."

Clara, Blizzard, and I took the old boat and puttered up to the new island wharf. Clara tied up with a perfect knot and I told her how much she'd grown in the two months I'd been gone.

We headed to the pasture where the herd was grazing. Blizzard trotted beside us but stayed close to me. "He missed you, Jessie," Clara told me. "We all did."

I caught sight of ripe blueberries bunched among the thick leaves of the bushes. "The berries are ripe."

Clara quickly picked a handful and placed them in my palm. We nibbled on them as we walked. I kept looking to see my Raven, but she wasn't in sight.

"Are you glad to be home?" Clara asked.

"Boston was fine. The buildings in the city were as high as our cliffs. I'm glad I went, but I'm right glad to be home again."

A fish hawk shrieked from high in the clouds, and in a nearby tree I heard the chitter-chatter of chickadees.

We had come to the place where someone—now I guessed it was probably Gran—had practiced shooting.

"Gran told me that nice girls don't shoot guns." Clara giggled. "I guess Gran wasn't a nice girl, then, was she?"

"She says nice girls don't drive boats or herd horses, either." My eyes scanned the pasture, then the barn. I could see ponies nibbling on grass and berries or just lying in the sunshine . . . but where was Raven?

Once we reached the pasture, we sat on a boulder. Blizzard lay on the ground near me. "Oh, there's Cocoa!" I pointed to the proud little stallion, who was grazing, his tail flicking at flies. "To think you were afeared of him."

"I was afeared of the fairies. Ma McCrumb used

to scare me all the time, tellin' me the fairies would come and get me."

"You'd be better off with fairies than with the McCrumbs."

"Gran says fairies are just a lot of pishogue."

"Gran's right. It's a whole lot of pishogue!"

"But Gran says angels aren't pishogue. They're real. Gran told me that the storm brought us angels: Uncle Don, and Ned . . ."

"Yes, they did turn out to be angels," I agreed, thinking how Uncle Don had helped us keep Clara. "And my friend-girls who rescued the ponies—they're angels too."

Clara threw her arms around me. "Gran says that you are *my* angel." She kissed me on the cheek.

"Gran said that?"

"Uh-huh." Clara looked over toward the horses. "Look, there's Raven." She pointed to a small hill where Raven stood watching us.

I stood up and called, "Raven! Come, girl, my good girl."

Raven's ears flicked at my voice, and she began to trot toward me. Suddenly, over the crest of the hill where she had been standing, I saw another smaller pony follow her. Raven waited for the little one to catch up to her on its lanky legs.

"A colt!" I cried. "Raven's had a colt!"

Clara giggled. "I couldn't wait to tell you, but everyone said it should be a surprise. It's a little girl. We think the dad is Cocoa."

As they came closer I could see that the foal had the same brown fur, dark mane, and sweet little mealy muzzle as Raven. She trotted close to her mother and watched us timidly.

Raven scurried up to me and nuzzled her head on my shoulder. "Oh, Raven, your baby is beautiful." The colt stayed right tight to Raven's side. "What's her name?" I asked Clara.

"We all agreed you should name her, Jessie."

For a long moment, as I stroked Raven's furry head and ears, I recalled all the loving, brave people who had helped save my little herd of ponies—my folks, Gran, Erik and Ned, Uncle Don, Sandra, Clara, Meta and the others . . . so many.

"I know just the name for this little colt," I finally said.

"What is it?" Clara asked eagerly.

"Her name is Angel," I told her.

AFTERWORD

Newfoundland is a large rocky island off the east coast of Canada. Labrador is located on the northeastern mainland, on the plateau known as the Canadian Shield. In 1949 the two together became the tenth province of Canada. The province of Newfoundland and Labrador is nicknamed "England's oldest colony—Canada's newest province."

The island of Newfoundland is a huge rock with towering cliffs. In fact, inhabitants lovingly refer to it as "the Beautiful Rock." For centuries the ponies helped the settlers of Newfoundland tame the rocky soil by plowing fields, hauling capelin and seaweed for fertilizer, dragging lumber from the forests, and serving the people in many other ways. The ponies became part of the history of Newfoundland.

Over the past fifty years or more, as the availability of cars, trucks, bulldozers, and other means of construction increased, the ponies were no longer used or needed. Many were left to fend for themselves and eventually to die of hunger. Some were trucked away to be used as human and animal food.

Because of the ponies' history of devotion and loyalty since they were first brought from the British Isles hundreds of years ago, they are now protected by provincial law. The Newfoundland Pony Society, a charitable organization, was formed to preserve, protect, and promote the Newfoundland pony as a distinct heritage animal. Shelters, such as the Change Islands Newfoundland Pony Refuge, are also dedicated to preserving this ancient breed of ponies. Families and organizations in Canada and the United States are also adopting ponies—just as in my story.

In the United States wild mustangs and burros face the same problems that the Newfoundland ponies face. Here, too, animal protection groups are fighting to protect the wild and beautiful mustangs and burros that are part of our history.

You've noticed, as you read my story, the colorful dialect that Newfoundlanders and Labradoreans speak, Newfoundland English, is derived from a mixture of English, French, and Gaelic. Many of the expressions I've used in my story are still heard in various parts of the island. I gathered them together to be used by my fictional characters in the imaginary setting of Gull Harbor and the Cliffs.

Remember how the Rideouts towed their house to Gull Harbor by boat? In the past, many small communities—known as outports—were scattered across hard-to-reach areas of the island. By the 1950s it had become difficult and expensive for the government to provide paved roads, electricity, schools, hospitals, and other services for so many regions. It was decided to relocate thousands of households by moving them from the distant bays and smaller islands to more central locations—providing the entire population of each settlement was in agreement. Families were paid for some of the costs of relocating. Many people (like the Rideouts in my story) wanted to bring their own houses, so they floated them or towed them to their new locations. Scenes of houses being hauled by manpower or trucks, or being towed in the harbor, became common sights as the resettlement program continued.

By 1975 the program had become so unpopular that it was allowed to fade out. Many folks moved back to the places of their birth and childhoods—back to the cliffs, bays, and islands they so dearly loved.

*   *   *

Read more about the Newfoundland pony at the Newfoundland Pony Society's website: www .newfoundlandpony.com.

The Newfoundland Pony: The Lone Member of the Moorland Family of Horses in North America, Now on the Verge of Extinction by Andrew F. Fraser is a comprehensive and interesting book that traces the history of the ponies. Dr. Fraser, a veterinarian and biologist, was the first President of the Newfoundland Pony Society.

Want to know more about the Newfoundland language? Check out the Newfoundland and Labrador Heritage site's Dictionary of Newfoundland English— and other heritage information! www.heritage.nf.ca /dictionary.

Did you know Newfoundland was discovered by Vikings five hundred years *before* Columbus "discovered" America? Visit L'Anse aux Meadows websites:
www.pc.gc.ca/lhn-nhs/nl/meadows/index_e.asp
www.cdli.ca/CITE/v_lanse.htm

ACKNOWLEDGMENTS

THANK YOU TO THE KEEPERS

Keeper of the Ponies:
Many thanks to Beverley Stevens and her Change Islands Newfoundland Pony Refuge in Change Islands, Newfoundland, for great pictures and information about the history of the Newfoundland ponies—and especially for her dedication to rescuing the ponies and to restoring this historic breed.

Keeper of Newfoundland History:
As always, quintals of gratitude go to my cousin and personal historian, Sandra Knight, who resides in Northwest Territories, but whose heart remains in Newfoundland. Thank you for sharing stories of our lovable, colorful, and hard-working families and their lives in Moreton's Harbor and Beachy Cove.

Keeper of Our Newfoundland Genealogy:
To Hugh Small, another cousin, who keeps remarkable records and photos of our mutual Newfoundland background—thank you, Hugh!

Keeper of the Spirit, Sentiment, and Memories:
To my talented cousin Larry Small, who wrote the beautiful book of poems *Around the Red Land*—many thanks for your gracious permission to quote a bit of "October Journey" in the preface of this book.

Keeper of the Site:
Thanks to Patty Roy—another family historian (and another cousin!)—who generously and brilliantly creates and manages my website.

Keepers of the Flame:
Deepest appreciation to my writing group—June, Carol, Elizabeth, and Gail—for their long-lasting friendship, critique, and inspiration, and for fanning the creative flame when it sometimes flickers.

Keeper of the Craft:
Much gratitude to my gifted editor, Lisa Cheng, for her skillful, adroit, and gentle editing of this story. It was a pleasure to work with you, Lisa.

Keeper of the Family Talent:
Thanks to my beautiful and talented daughter,

Kristan Johnson, for coming up with the delightful title, *Secret of the Night Ponies.*

Keeper of the Promise:
As Newfoundland's heritage of cod and capelin, flakes and stages, schooners and sails, fish and brewis, gardens and horses fades into history, I'm hoping my "yarns" will keep the old Newfoundland alive in the hearts and imaginations of children—and perhaps *they* will be the Keepers of the Promise.